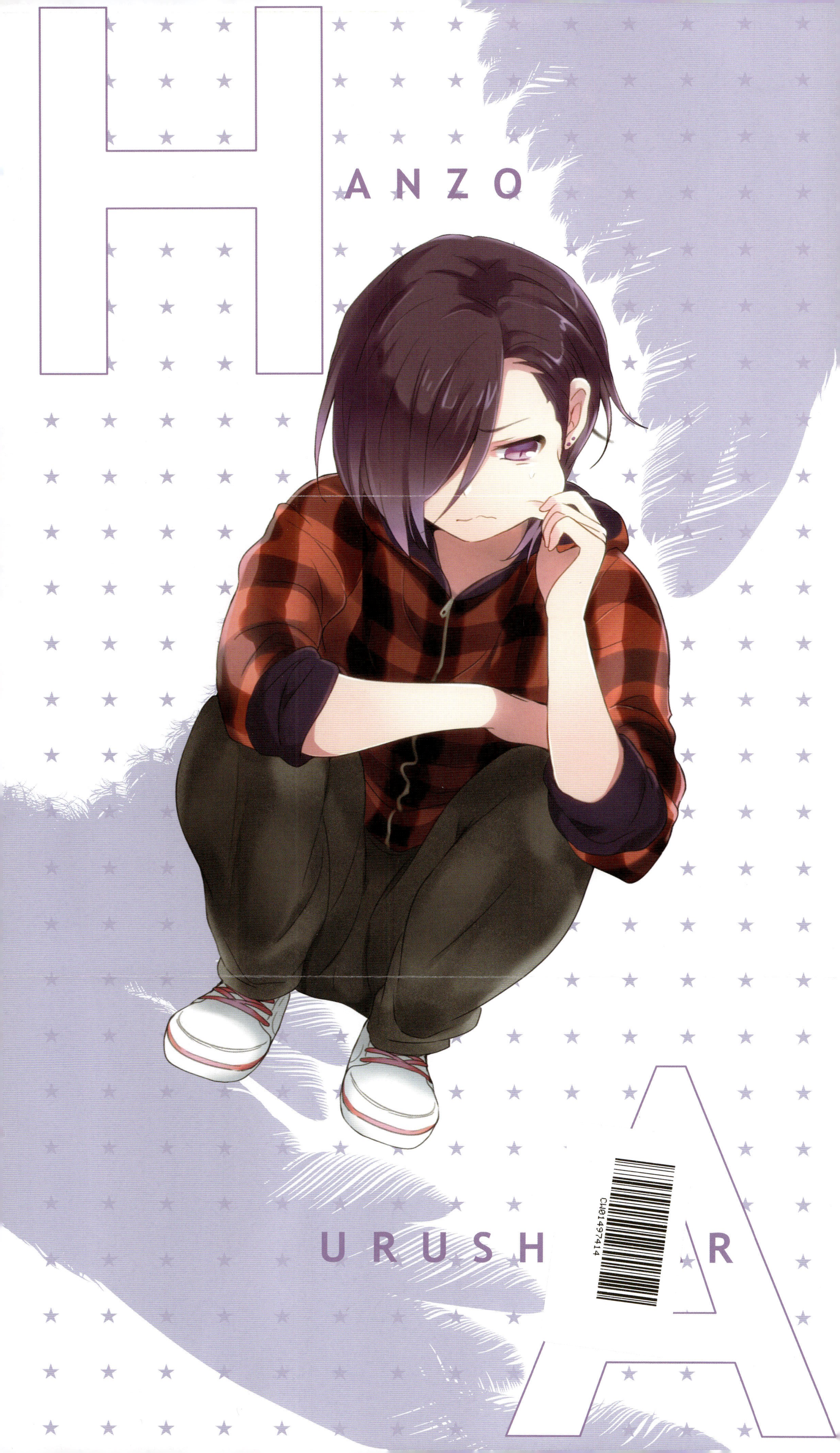
HANZO
URUSH
A
R
CW01497414

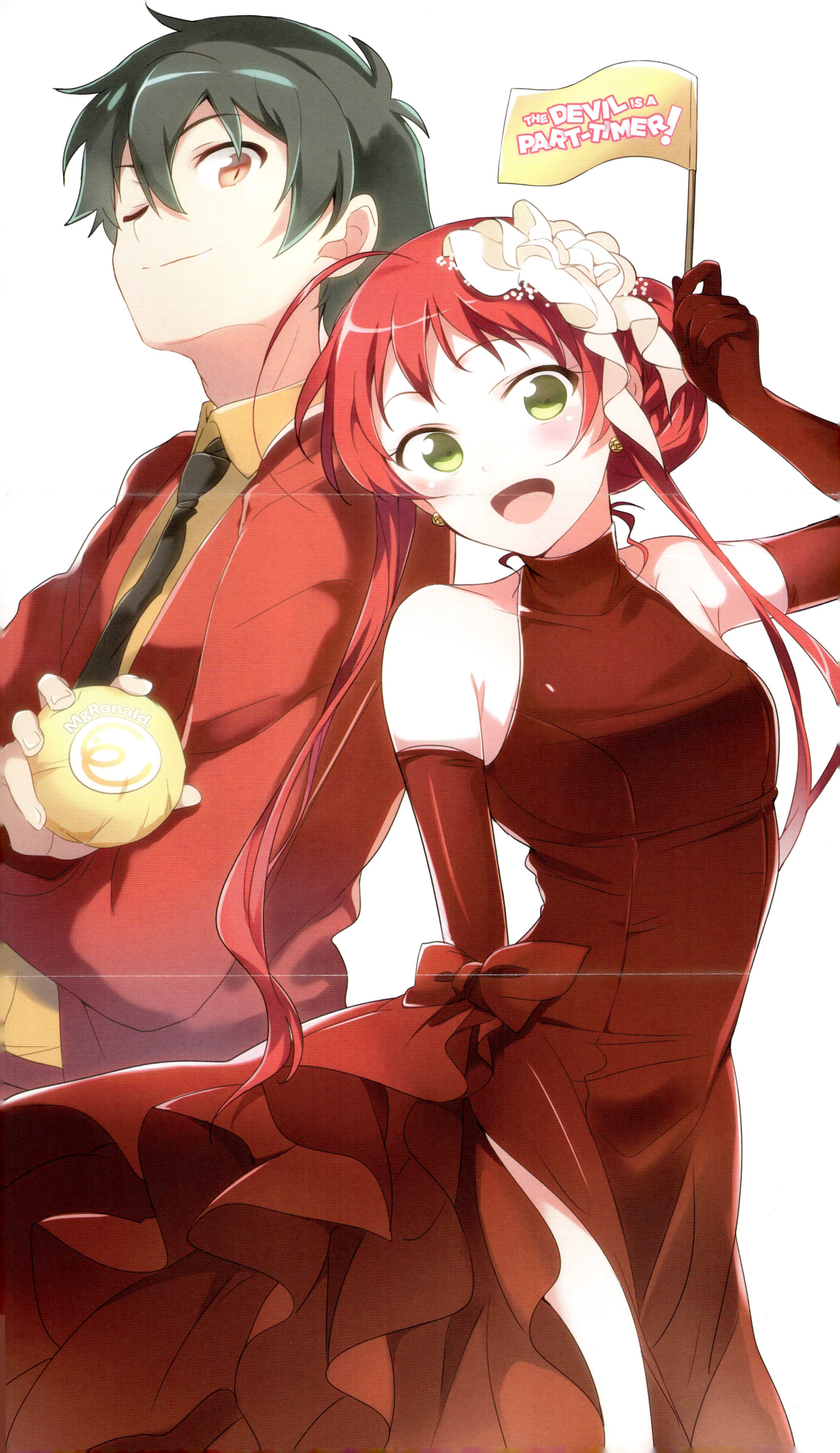
THE DEVIL IS A PART-TIMER!
MgRonald.

THE DEVIL IS A PART-TIMER!

15

SATOSHI
WAGAHARA
ILLUSTRATION BY
029 (ONIKU)

MgRonald's

CONTENTS

THE DEVIL IS A PART-TIMER!

SATOSHI WAGAHARA
ILLUSTRATED BY ■ 029 (ONIKU)

15

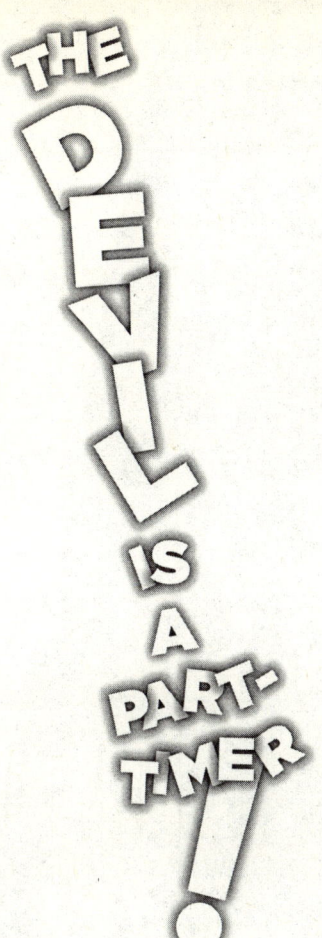

YEN ON
NEW YORK

THE DEVIL IS A PART-TIMER!, Volume 15
SATOSHI WAGAHARA, ILLUSTRATION BY 029 (ONIKU)

Translation by Kevin Gifford
Cover art by 029 (oniku)

HATARAKU MAOUSAMA!, Volume 15
© SATOSHI WAGAHARA 2016
Edited by Dengeki Bunko

First published in Japan in 2016 by KADOKAWA CORPORATION, Tokyo.
English translation rights arranged with KADOKAWA CORPORATION,
Tokyo, through Tuttle-Mori Agency, Inc., Tokyo.

English translation © 2019 by Yen Press, LLC

Yen On
150 West 30th Street, 19th Floor
New York, NY 10001

Visit us at yenpress.com
facebook.com/yenpress
twitter.com/yenpress
yenpress.tumblr.com
instagram.com/yenpress

First Yen On Edition: December 2019

Yen On is an imprint of Yen Press, LLC.
The Yen On name and logo are trademarks of Yen Press, LLC.

The publisher is not responsible for websites (or their
content) that are not owned by the publisher.

Library of Congress Cataloging-in-Publication Data
Names: Wagahara, Satoshi. | 029 (Light novel illustrator)
illustrator. | Gifford, Kevin, translator. | Steinbach, Kevin,
translator.
Title: The devil is a part-timer! / Satoshi Wagahara ;
illustration by 029 (oniku) ; translation by Kevin Gifford;
translation by Kevin Steinbach.
Other titles: Hataraku Maousama!. English
Description: First Yen On edition. | New York, NY :
Yen On, 2015–
Identifiers: LCCN 2015028390 |
ISBN 9780316388127 (v. 1 : pbk.) |
ISBN 9780316385015 (v. 2 : pbk.) |
ISBN 9780316385022 (v. 3 : pbk.) |
ISBN 9780316385039 (v. 4 : pbk.) |
ISBN 9780316385046 (v. 5 : pbk.) |
ISBN 9780316385060 (v. 6 : pbk.) |
ISBN 9780316469364 (v. 7 : pbk.) |
ISBN 9780316473910 (v. 8 : pbk.) |
ISBN 9780316474184 (v. 9 : pbk.) |
ISBN 9780316474207 (v. 10 : pbk.) |
ISBN 9780316474238 (v. 11 : pbk.) |
ISBN 9780316474252 (v. 12 : pbk.) |
ISBN 9781975302658 (v. 13 : pbk.) |
ISBN 9781975302672 (v. 14 : pbk.) |
ISBN 9781975302696 (v. 15 : pbk.)
Subjects: CYAC: Fantasy.
Classification: LCC PZ7.1.W34 Ha 2015 | DDC
[Fic]—dc23
LC record available at
http://lccn.loc.gov/2015028390

ISBNs: 978-1-9753-0269-6 (paperback)
978-1-9753-0270-2 (ebook)

1 3 5 7 9 10 8 6 4 2

LSC-C

Printed in the United States of America

PROLOGUE: THE TEEN AND THE CALL-CENTER LADY RING IN THE NEW YEAR

It was a quiet morning, the early sunlight giving form to the assorted things that keep the world going in the dark. These could be people; these could be buildings; these could be roads; these could be towns—and this was the light of life for it all, which drove them forward and all but dared them to shine the night away. This light and sound were the breath of existence for them, and any place without them was an inscrutable, fluid object, like a flatly colored shadow. An oven without any gas, a dried-up well—or a building with no one in it.

"You have to be kidding me," said the shaky voice of a woman, making the morning light almost quiver with her heavy breath. "This has to be a joke."

"It doesn't appear to be," another voice replied, also a little unsure of itself as its owner solemnly surveyed what lay ahead of her—a sight that would even make the morning sunrise freeze in place. "There's nobody in the whole apartment."

"This is kind of a mean prank..."

The two women, in their own individual ways, were appraising the scene inside the building they stood before—Villa Rosa Sasazuka, a postwar-era wooden apartment building in the Sasazuka neighborhood of Tokyo's Shibuya district. The time was about to pass eight in the morning, but there was not a single sign of life inside.

"So did they all…uh, leave?"

"Yeah."

"What about Emi's father? He's on the first floor, right?"

"Gone."

"Suzuno?"

"Gone."

"What about Maou? And Urushihara?"

"…Both gone."

"And…Ashiya?"

"Rika." Chiho Sasaki sternly put an end to Rika Suzuki's broken-record act. "Please understand. For the moment the apartment complex is…completely empty."

"Why…? But why?!!" Rika shook her head, trying to stave off the unbelievable truth. "That can't…be? I mean, all this time, nobody… nobody said…anything…?"

She looked up at the deserted Villa Rosa Sasazuka, her voice trailing off. Then she turned her eyes back toward Chiho.

"Wh-what about Emi? Emi's got to be here, right?! In Eifukucho! She wouldn't be here anyway—"

"Yusa is gone, too."

"No way!"

Rika's shriek did nothing to break the look on Chiho's face.

"Alas Ramus and Acieth can't leave Yusa and Maou's side, either," she said before driving the final nail into the coffin. "They all went back…to Ente Isla."

"Oh, no…"

Ente Isla. The homeland of Chiho Sasaki and Rika Suzuki's most cherished of friends, a world far away from Sasazuka or Tokyo or Japan—or Earth, for that matter. And now Chiho was telling her these friends had all ventured off to the other end of the galaxy, a place normal, unassuming human beings like them could never reach.

"So… That's it? They're gone?"

"Yeah."

"But… Like, what about Maou's and Emi's jobs…?"

Rika sounded ready to burst into tears as Chiho shook her head. "Did you think they'd just go without telling anyone? It's already all been worked out."

Leaving the side of her confused companion, Chiho breathed a sigh, breath visible in the air, and stepped onto the apartment's front lawn. Frost from the morning was still visible in the shaded areas of the lot, leaving clear footprints wherever Chiho's sneakers landed.

"And it's not just them, either," she said, after closing her eyes for a moment at the stairway landing. "Emeralda, Laila, Gabriel… All of them. You won't find any of them in Japan."

There was a rasp to her voice, as if she had yet to fully accept this truth herself.

"And Erone, and Amane, and the landlord… They're all in Ente Isla, too."

"But… Amane doesn't even have anything to do with that planet! Aren't the angels supposed to be gunning for Maou's and Emi's lives?!"

"Well, if you're someone from the Ente Isla side, then the lives of the Sephirah—of Alas Ramus, and Acieth, and Erone, and everyone else—they take precedent above all that."

Chiho took a leather key holder out from her coat pocket. Three dials were poised on one side of it, each labeled with a little sticker reading "101," "201," and "202," in Chiho's handwriting.

"Is that…?"

"The keys to their rooms," Chiho agreed as she began to climb the stairs, a flustered Rika following her. She stopped upon reaching Room 201 and took out the key to the apartment, not even bothering to ring the bell or shout hello to anyone.

"I— Oh no…"

The sight on the other side of the door made Rika fall to her knees. Room 201 was barren. It wasn't just a case of the residents being out on an errand—there was nothing. Not a single pot or ladle sat in the kitchen that used to be Ashiya's command center, and both

Urushihara's desk and the computer that sat on it were gone. The hastily assembled low table, where Chiho sat together with Maou and all her many other friends so often, was nowhere to be found. Now there was just a hundred or so square feet of empty space, no evidence of life or humanity. It was bleak inside, the stains on the ceiling, marks on the walls, and faded tatami-mat floor making it seem even bleaker.

"We're just normal people. We're not able to fight like they can. And you know all Maou and Yusa want is to keep us from getting hurt. So..."

So there was no way to join the fight in Ente Isla—a battle that featured an entire world waging war against its own deities.

"But...but *this* is what they do with us?"

A single tear fell from the corner of Rika's eye. She wasn't strong enough to take the suddenness and unfairness of it. Knowing the truth about Maou and everyone else and loving them for it anyway made it impossible.

"You're...fine with this, Chiho?"

"..."

"This is really okay with you?"

Rika's voice was chiding, as well it should be. Chiho had known them all for much longer; they had valued her as a person, no matter what world or race she had come from. It was only natural, Chiho supposed, that Rika would expect her to do something about this.

"How?" she replied in a low voice. "How could this *ever* be...okay with me...?"

"...!"

Then, for the first time, Rika spotted the quivering of Chiho's lips, the shaking in her balled-up fists. No, it could never be okay. But she accepted these facts anyway. And Rika needed to understand how much resolve and courage and grief it took for her to accept these apartment keys instead.

"...I'm sorry. I..."

"It'd never be okay with me..." Chiho repeated, her voice blankly echoing against the snuffed-out shell of Room 201.

* * *

The planet was no longer playing home to visitors from another world. They were back where they belonged—away from Earth, and Japan, and Chiho's and Rika's lives. But the typical, familiar rhythm of their lives before they discovered the truth was something neither of them were prepared to slip back into again.

Why did this have to happen? It was January 3, a time when Japan was still filled with traditional New Year's decorations and traditions. The curtain was rising on a brand-new year, but for Chiho and Rika, the way ahead seemed cloaked in despair.

And as Chiho looked down at the slumped-over Rika and reflected on the path Maou and his friends took to this war between gods, angels, and devils, all she could think was *Why did this have to happen?*

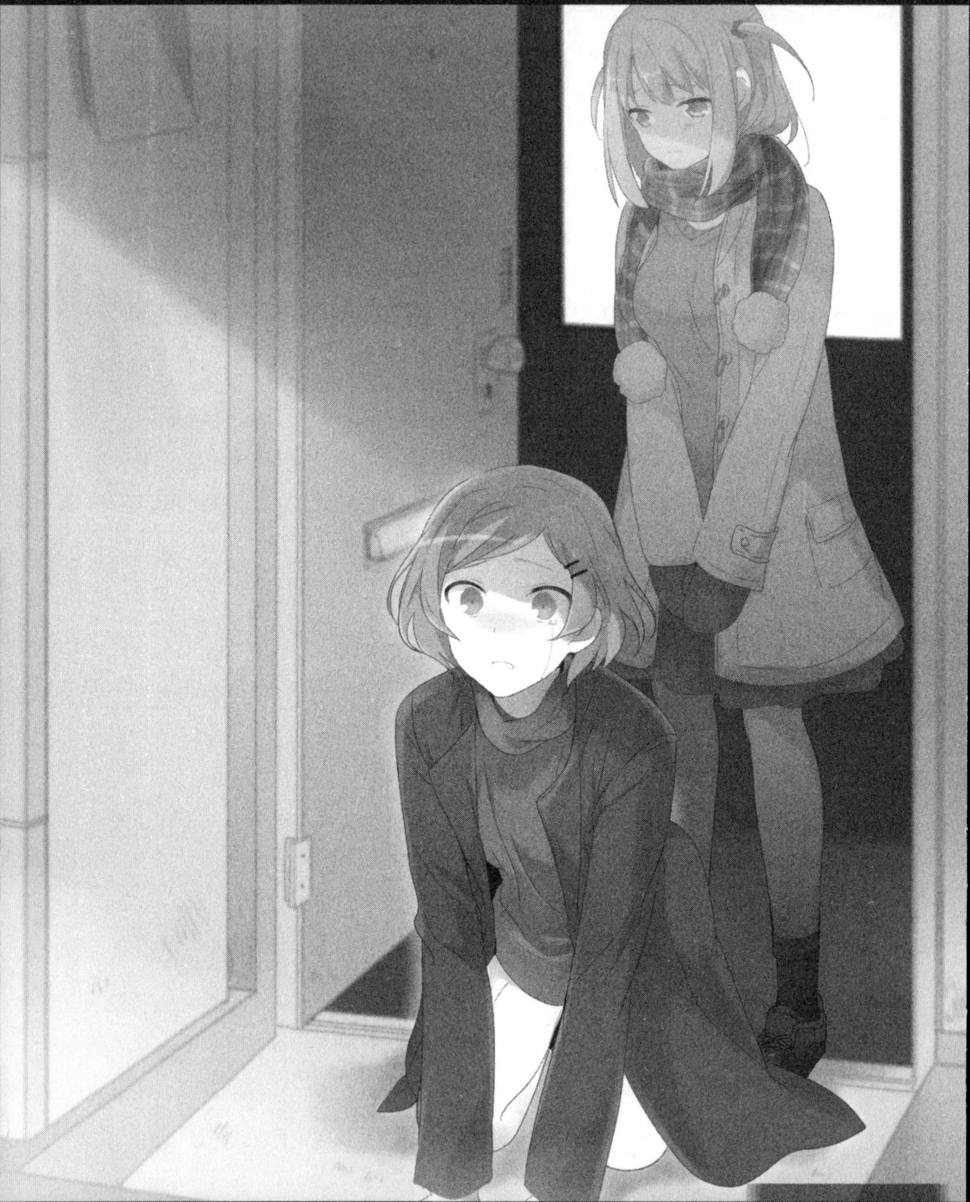

THE DEVIL KING IS OUT OF THE OFFICE (1)

"I…I can't believe it."

"Well, I mean…"

Chiho awkwardly turned her face away, unable to bear the strain of such cold, accusatory eyes upon her. But Kaori Shoji, her classmate, *kyudo* archery partner, and close friend, simply leaned closer.

"Hey, can you say that again? 'Cause I sure didn't believe it the first time."

"Well, that is…"

"What's up with your work shift?"

"Ahh…"

Chiho was now leaning back in her seat. Kaori gave her no quarter.

"Christmas Eve! What's up with your work shift that day?!"

"Umm," Chiho replied, noticing her friend's flared nostrils. "So Maou's working, Yusa's working, and I'm spending it at home with my family."

"Come *onnnnnn*, Sasachi!"

"Aggghhh…"

Still looming over the poor girl, Kaori now had her by the collar of her shirt, shaking her around.

"So what about the day of?" she asked, all but mounting the desk that separated them. "What about the twenty-fifth?!"

"L-let me go! I can't breathe!"

Chiho tried to shake Kaori off. Kaori just glared back. No mercy would be offered until she had her answer—and that's what made it so hard to give. She was gonna be *so* mad.

"All three of us are working that day…"

"Until when?!"

"……………………………Ten PM for me, until closing for them."

"Come *onnnnnnnnnnnnnnnnnnnnnn*, Sasachi!"

The scream rose in a crescendo, as Chiho desperately tried to push Kaori back before she vaulted the desk entirely and fell on the floor.

"What am I *supposed* to do about it? I'm too young to work past ten!"

"That's not the problem!" Kaori shouted, spraying a big wad of spittle from the corner of her mouth. "What made you ever agree to that shift in the first place?! What are you even thinking?! I mean, I can't even explain to you how much of a shock this is! Last time was *nothing* compared to this!" She hung her head in her hands, groaning. "Well, fine. Fine. Go ahead! Celebrate Christmas with your family! A lot of people *do* that, and I am, too! But this time… *This* time, like, *this*, of all years, that's totally the wrong thing to do!"

"You think…? But we're gonna be short-staffed between Christmas and New Year's…"

"Look, I don't care if people think teens these days are all lazy and stuff; I'm *never* gonna take a job where I have to work around New Year's! It's stupid MgRonald's fault for bothering to be open!"

Chiho, no doubt spoiled a bit by the serene comfort of Japan's modern culture of convenience, felt like arguing against this. She fought back the impulse.

"Look, Sasachi, listen to me for a moment."

"Um, yes?"

"You told me a while back that you wanted Maou to give you an answer, right?"

"Huh? Ah, um, yeah."

Having this topic broached out of nowhere made Chiho scope out her classroom surroundings. Kaori's acrobatics were over now, so everyone around them had stopped paying attention. But given how her classmates were just the right age to latch on to topics like this, Chiho didn't want anyone eavesdropping on them. Kaori knew that full well, of course, but apparently she just *had* to ask right now.

"Come on, Sasachi. We're teenage girls, right? Teenage girls. It's right about the time we want a little more drama in our lives, like grown-ups have."

"I—I guess…"

In terms of drama, Chiho was confident that, in the past year, she had had more of that and change than most Hollywood celebrities, hands down. She was fine with her current portion, thank you very much, but she gave a meek nod anyway.

"So what's with this act of yours, huh? The one day you get a better shot at that drama than any other day of the year, and you're going to leave your main rival alone with the guy you love so you can entertain at home with your parents? You really think you're in that good of a position here?"

"Yusa's not my 'main rival' or anything…"

"Oh, hush! Anyone but you can see she totally is!" She pointed an accusatory finger like a lecturing sister-in-law. "I'm assuming you haven't drummed up the guts to ask for a reply yet. Wouldn't you normally try to settle things with him on Christmas Eve, then? The one day you got for it?"

Chiho could tell what Kaori meant. The thought hadn't completely escaped her mind. But…

"But I mean, December's schedule was already set up since last month, when we talked about it, so…"

"Nooooo, this won't work! It won't, it won't! It won't work at all! You got no chance whatsoever, Sasachi. You could wait five hundred years and not get an answer! Just give up! Give up."

"But—but that's…"

Kaori's head was back in her hands.

Chiho hadn't been totally oblivious. As the sights and sounds of town began to take on a holiday theme, she had dreamed about going on a nice Christmas date with Maou somewhere. She had dreamed about it, but this was the Lord of All Demons, and as far as she knew, this would be his second Christmas in Japan. She didn't know how the last one went for him, but chances were he was working—and this year, yes, he had picked up a full MgRonald shift on the twenty-fourth *and* the twenty-fifth.

✳

She had actually realized she might be missing the chance of a lifetime back at the end of November. The shifts were long set in stone; asking Maou or Ms. Kisaki for a shift change around the holiday was unthinkable.

Things had been pretty chaotic between September and November for both Chiho and everyone involved with Ente Isla, with Emi and Ashiya being captured, Maou sallying forth to rescue them, Urushihara having a stint in the hospital, and Emi's mother appearing out of nowhere. It had been particularly rough for Emi, being reunited with a mom whom she hardly remembered but who had laid such a heavy burden upon both her and the entire world.

Both Laila—archangel and Emi's mother—and Sadao Maou, the Demon Lord who Chiho loved, had clearly taken great pains to lighten Emi's heart during all this, despite the fact that Laila and Maou could hardly be said to get along. It was a gesture Chiho, who cared about both sides of that equation deeply, should have been glad for—but, as she now realized, seeing Maou treat Emi with kindness made her terribly jealous.

For better or for worse, his attitude toward Chiho hadn't changed since summer, when she first confessed her love. If he and Emi were to accept the "big job" Laila brought to their attention, they would go very, very far away from Chiho. She had no idea how to grasp the relationship between herself and this guy from another world—so she had asked her friend Kaori Shoji for advice, leaving out the extraneous Ente Isla–related details.

That had happened at the end of November, and even by then, there was no way she could do anything as bold as ask for a Christmas date. But something else now disturbed her just as much: Rika Suzuki, friend to Emi and another acquaintance who knew the truth behind their little social circle, had confessed her own interests to Shirou Ashiya, the Great Demon General Alciel. She had opened her heart to him—but it hadn't been enough.

To Chiho, Rika seemed like a superstar: falling in love with an Ente Islan, not letting that truth faze her, and actually *saying* her feelings instead of running away from them. She was just that—a great, shining star—and it scared Chiho. The mere thought of Maou turning her down after all this made her legs shake. She could imagine a million reasons why Maou might say no, but—for now at least—not a single reason for him to say yes.

Rika hadn't given up after Ashiya's refusal. She had cried about it, but she never gave up. However, imagining herself in that same situation, Chiho didn't know how she'd ever manage to recover if Maou refused her. Maybe throughout the last few weeks, she had been unconsciously trying to avoid thinking about Christmas at all.

Whatever Maou's choice was, it would have to be directly linked with his other future decisions. That future involved far more than her—it could mean that Chiho lost not just Maou but Emi, Ashiya, Urushihara, Suzuno, and all her other Ente Islan friends. That puppylike drive to not be away from the one she loved for a single moment froze her, preventing any action.

But at the same time, Chiho had another voice running through her mind: *If there is something to say, just say it fast or else lots of regrets.*

These were the words of Acieth Alla, a girl separated from her own companions for eons longer than a seventeen-year-old girl could ever imagine—but Chiho still understood the portent behind them.

She knew Kaori, and she knew Acieth, too. And that was what made Chiho's own heart freeze in place, descended upon by thick clouds and preventing any movement.

Such were Chiho's mid-December days.

※

"Don't just say 'but—but'! I can't believe you let Christmas just slip through your fingers like that!"

Kaori couldn't be blamed for seeing all this as Chiho just screwing up a chance at having a hot guy in her life. But to Chiho, the things she *was* letting "slip through" made something as inconsequential as a romantic Christmas impossible to think about.

"Can you do anything else at this point?" Kaori asked. "We've got a little time until Christmas. Could you find someone to cover your shifts?"

"Ooh, I dunno…"

It was the obvious question to pose, in a way, and Chiho had thought about it. But while she could maybe jump off a shift she was assigned to, getting someone else to take one for her sake was another matter. And there was no way Chiho could ask Maou, of all people, to take off Christmas Eve so they could take care of some business.

"Oh, wait! Maybe I could tell my mom that we're short-staffed and go in on the twenty-fourth, too…"

"Sasachi, why is *that* what you're coming up with at this point?"

"Huh? What's wrong with it?"

"What's wrong? Everything! You go to work that day, and it'll be just another shift, from start to finish! Plus, you'll still have to go home before he does, right? Are you even serious about this, Sasachi?"

"S-serious?"

"*You're* the one who was all like, *Ooh, I don't wanna drift away from them!* Well, guess what? You're already, like, half faded out from the picture!"

"Well, yeah, I guess I know that, but…"

If Maou and friends accepted Laila's plea to save the people of Ente Isla, it'd be just like when Maou set off to rescue Emi before. Chiho, in other words, wouldn't be along for the ride—or couldn't be, really. The reason was simple: If things erupted into war, she'd be a drag on Maou and Emi, like she always was. They were fighting against a total unknown, in a number of ways. Bringing the totally defenseless Chiho into that war zone would force Maou's side to devote too many resources to protecting her. It wouldn't be like before, when she used the Yesod to take advantage of Laila's force for a while. Laila had made herself known to them all, and now that she had, there was no good reason for Chiho to fight alongside Maou.

But somewhere in her heart, Chiho couldn't deny that Kaori was right. She did have a little time, and she had ample reason to believe Maou wouldn't return to Ente Isla that easily. That was because, on a wholly different dimension from what Laila had offered him, he had another huge job offer potentially in the works.

"…But if the shifts are all set up, no changing them now, huh? Well, are you at least thinking about stuff you could do for the thirty-first or New Year's?"

"Oh, I think my mom or dad were saying something about going back to my grandparents' place, so…um…Kao?"

Chiho was so occupied thinking about Maou's current situation that she hardly noticed how Kaori was staring at her like a cobra ready to strike. Demons struck her with less terror than what she now felt.

"Sasachi…"

"Y-yes?"

"I'm seriously angry now."

She had been seriously angry enough before, but Chiho was too cowed to offer any complaint about the torrent of sass and lecturing that followed.

It was already dark by the time archery practice was over.

Chiho wasn't working today, so she was on her way home when she received a text from her mother, directing her into the crowds at the 100 Trees Shopping Arcade. The whole outdoor mall was set up in holiday colors, although some of the shops had already taken down the red bows and replaced them with New Year's décor—the specialty food, fish, and noodle shops in particular.

"Oh, Chiho Sasaki?"

She was reading over the impromptu shopping list her mother had texted her when she heard a wholly unexpected voice in the crowd. It almost made her drop her phone. "Huh... Whaaa?!"

She turned around and received another shock. It *wasn't* just her ears playing tricks on her.

"U-Urushihara?! Since when did you get out?"

He winced at this appraisal, not that he had much to defend himself with. "Dude, don't make it sound like I'm a violent felon just outta prison."

"Yeah, but I mean, I couldn't even imagine you released to the general public on your own recognizance like this..."

"Look, do you guys think I'm some kinda wild animal or zombie or something? Maybe you didn't notice, but I've been going out alone a lot lately, and I even picked up a job or two back at the apartment."

"Wow, really? Um, I'm sorry..." Chiho bowed. Maybe "released" was going a little too far.

Thinking about it, though, this was the first time she had seen the former angel outside without Maou or Ashiya accompanying him since back in the spring, right when she had learned the truth about all of them. It wasn't pure laziness, she recalled, that kept him from leaving the apartment.

"But, um, are you sure you're okay going around alone?"

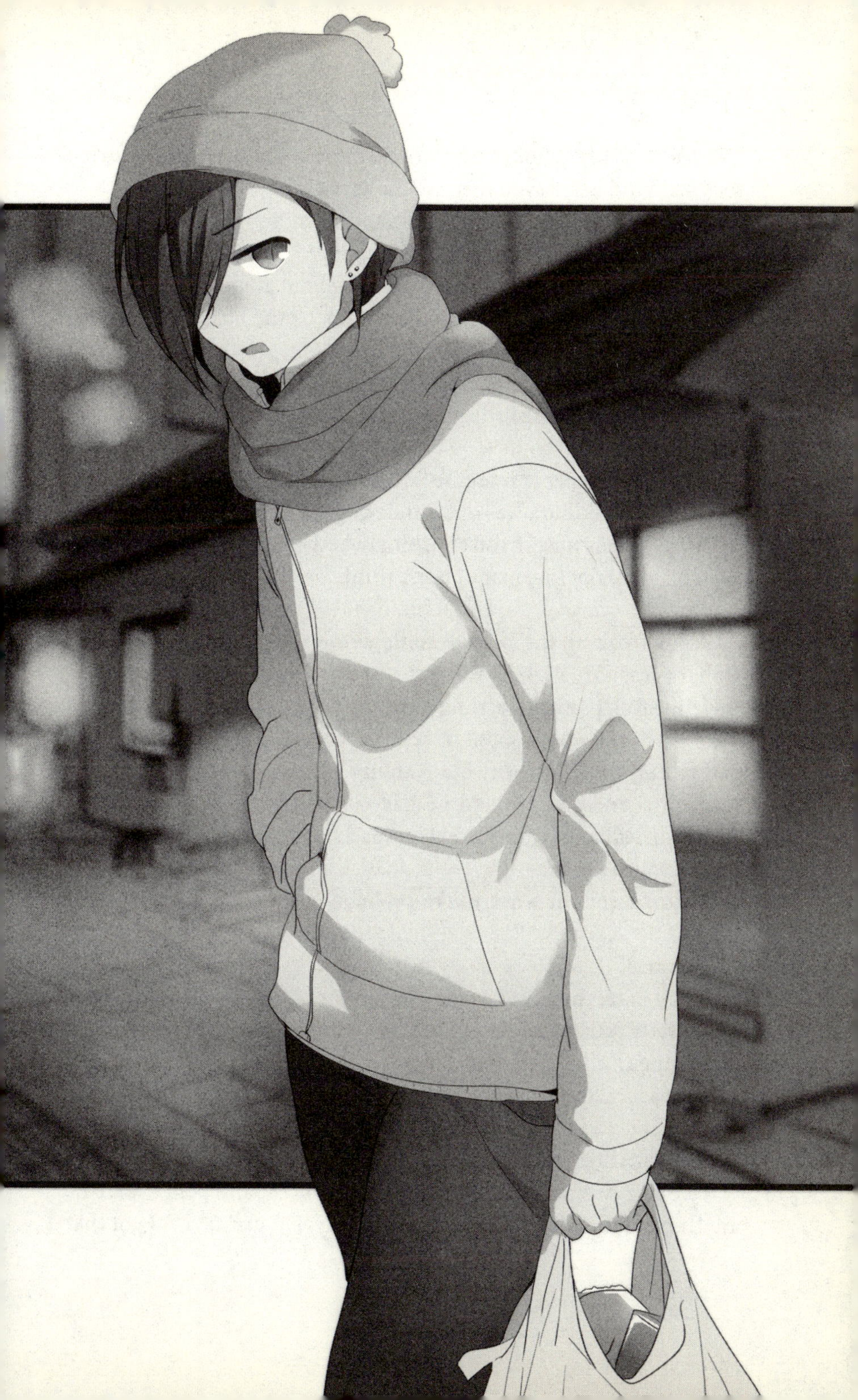

"Meaning, like, should I be worried about the cops arresting me for what I did before you met us?" he asked.

"Huh? Oh, yeah…I guess…" Chiho raised an eyebrow. His tone sounded odd to her. He clicked his tongue.

"Yeah, like, Bell said that basically if I go out alone, I'd be screwed and maybe I wouldn't even make it back to the apartment in one piece, so…"

"Yes…"

"Hey, don't just agree with that."

"S-sorry…"

It was easy for her to imagine Suzuno saying something like that if she knew Urushihara was out wandering the town alone.

"Yeah, so anyway, if you're asking whether it's okay or not, then it's still not really that okay, I don't think."

"Oh?"

Chiho froze at the breezy confession. A big reason why Urushihara was largely housebound was that, in the period between traveling to Japan and settling down in Villa Rosa Sasazuka, he had essentially gone on a spree of serial robberies. Chiho didn't know everything he had done, but judging by how Maou and Ashiya reacted, chances were good he had committed at least one crime near a surveillance camera. There was a nonzero chance he was still on the police's radar.

"But in terms of what *you're* probably worried about, I bet I'm fine."

"You are?"

"Yeah. Like, thanks to Maou, we got enough demonic force that I have pretty much free rein to use it. A buncha cops don't scare me." He grinned.

"Whoa, don't say *that*!"

There was something devilish about Urushihara's smile that made Chiho, daughter of a police officer, panic.

"Hee-hee-hee! I'm not planning to rub out Japan's police force or anything, dude. But if things get real hairy, I'm just sayin', I got that on my side and a lot of other things going besides that. I feel really good right now, y'know? Gettin' to tackle all this new stuff."

"A lot of other things"? "All this new stuff"? Chiho was too scared to ask for specifics, but given the demons' activities over the past few months, she could make a few assumptions. And although Urushihara didn't mean to, his remarks gave Chiho a hint about something that had been on her mind for a while now.

"So that means you have demonic force again, too, Urushihara?"

"What d'you mean 'too'?" he asked, the grin still on his face.

Chiho responded with a confident smirk of her own, as she revealed a couple of facts she knew.

"Well, Ashiya is walking around with his own, yeah? Enough to go back into demon form whenever he wants."

"Oh, you knew that? Like, what happened the day he bought the phone?"

"…More or less, yeah." Chiho was more than a bit interested in Urushihara's take on that day's events.

"But… Huh," he muttered. "How d'you know about that, though? 'Cause Bell sure doesn't seem to know."

"That's because I didn't say anything about it."

"Oh? 'Cause, I mean, dude, I know you. If you knew we were keeping demonic force hidden from Emilia and stuff, I figured you'd be so freaked out you'd run over to her for advice."

Chiho grimaced. "You don't have to act like I'm a double agent or something. I know full well Ashiya isn't the type of person who'd go around like that for no reason."

There were other reasons why she had never told Emi and Suzuno, but being treated like a tattletale irked her a little.

"Huh. So maybe Emilia doesn't know, either? Hmm."

Urushihara nodded, not letting on whether this meant something to him or if he was just stringing the conversation along. He raised a hand into the air. Chiho had been too amazed by Urushihara's mere presence to notice, but it was holding a plastic shopping bag filled with snacks, dinner items, and more.

"I mean, I figured Emilia woulda known once Ashiya decided to transform in front of Rika Suzuki, but... Ah, it doesn't really matter if she knows anyway. Like you said, we ain't doing this for no reason, and it also connects to this shopping run I'm on."

"...What do you mean?"

"Mmm..."

Urushihara carefully looked around at his surroundings. Finding a nearby café, he pointed it out to Chiho.

"I'll tell you if you buy me something hot to drink. I'm cold."

"..."

Chiho raised her eyebrows up in a *really?* look before grudgingly nodding. In the end, it turned out this really was the same shameless Urushihara as always.

"It's really nothing big," the fallen angel began, sipping from the most expensive seasonal coffee special on the menu. "It's just that Maou, Ashiya, and I don't fully trust Laila yet."

"Don't fully trust her?" Chiho asked as she dumped a generous portion of milk into a cup of the cheapest house blend on offer. "What's that mean?"

"Exactly what it sounds like, my dudette. She's been on the run from heaven for ages now, right? But she's leaving herself super wide-open in all this. She's making both Maou *and* Emilia worry about her."

"Yeah, she is." Chiho immediately nodded. Even she could tell that Laila was doing herself no favors.

"Just because Gabriel and our landlord said that heaven closed off all Gate access to and from itself doesn't mean we know that for sure. It being closed doesn't guarantee our enemy's stuck there. Maybe it's more of a one-way thing, where they can keep sending people on down from above. We're not willing to believe that Laila's keeping everything perfectly balanced for herself here. You remember how me and Ashiya didn't join you guys when you went to Laila's place?"

"Oh, right, you didn't."

Laila had opened up her apartment in the Nerima district to them, in an attempt to gain their trust. Ashiya and Urushihara declined to tag along, and given that Rika's utter failure at a love confession took place just the day before, Chiho had been reluctant to ask why at the time.

"Yeah. And I mean, personally, I really don't care about Laila's place. But that was all Maou's idea."

"Maou's idea?"

"Yeah, like, *you stay behind in case something happens.* Like, if worse comes to worst and the enemy takes advantage of a distracted Maou and Emilia to attack MgRonald or Rika Suzuki, or hell, even your house or whatever, we could instantly respond to it that way."

"…Oh."

"Plus, all that woe-is-me crap from Laila might've just been her trying to pull on Maou's and Emilia's heartstrings. So it might be more than just Raguel and Camael we have to deal with."

"Huh?"

Chiho had trouble understanding Urushihara's point. He responded with a disdainful snort.

"Like, my dudette, why are we assuming Laila's one of the good guys just because she's Emilia's mom? None of that seems weird to you? I mean, not that I'm one to talk, but are *any* of the angels you know good guys so far, Chiho Sasaki?"

"No."

Sadly, she could instantly reply to that.

"Right, see? And I'm totally not one to talk, but I kinda got a perspective on angelic assholery that Maou and Ashiya don't have. What if all that airheaded screwing around on her part's just an act? What if she tries to use your family or the MgRonald manager or Rika Suzuki or someone else important to Maou or Emilia as hostages, so those two'll do what she wants them to? 'Cause the chance of that is a lot higher than none, y'know?"

This sounded like the kind of four-dimensional subterfuge Laila didn't exactly seem capable of engineering, but Urushihara's point made sense.

"Well, what do you think, Urushihara? About her?"

"What do I think?" he quickly countered, not giving away the slightest hint of his impression. It forced Chiho to be more specific.

"I mean, Laila and Gabriel... They want Maou and everyone to, uh, kill her, right, umm..."

"Oh, right, you heard about my parents, huh?"

"............Heard about them, yeah."

His addressing it straight like that threw her a little.

"So you gonna treat me with a little more respect now?"

"Uh, what?"

Chiho was floored at this sudden change of subject. How did that connect to anything?

"I mean, look at this crazy pedigree I got! My mom's literally a god. Head of the second generation of angels. If she was human, she'd be so high up, you'd be afraid to even look at her."

It was hard to tell how serious he was being. Chiho felt the need to address him honestly anyway. "Can you stop being ridiculous and answer my question?"

"Dude, you're even pickier about that stuff than Emilia is, huh? Well, all right. I give up. I mean, really, you guys can do whatever you want. If Maou believes Laila's really being sincere about this and says yes, then I'm not gonna try and stop them."

"Are you sure?! Because, I mean..."

"Yeah, I know, I know. They're trying to kill my mother in heaven, right? Laila, and Gabriel, and somebody else for all we know." Urushihara's voice was just as flat and monotone as his facial expression. "Or what, you think I'm suddenly gonna start loving my mom and tearfully plead for her life? Or like, suddenly change myself entirely at this point to bring her on to our side?"

"No, I'm not thinking the second thing at all, but it's odd to hear you be so disinterested in her."

"Man, you guys think you can just say whatever you want about me, huh? Well, come over to the apartment sometime, dudette. I think you're gonna be surprised." Urushihara winced again.

"Ughh… I mean, I'm not lying or whatever when I say this, but I really don't remember my parents much at all. I know as a fact that Ignora, ruler of the heavens, is my mother, and I kind of have these vague memories of her, but if you're asking me whether she has any impact on my life as it stands, the answer's a big fat no."

"Oh…"

It was hard to believe for someone with as healthy a family life as Chiho's. But Urushihara didn't seem to be acting.

"I mean, I don't live in this dimension where we have feelings for each other for no reason, just because she's my mom and I'm her son or whatever. In the demon realms, if your dad or your brother gets in your way, you kill him. It's that simple. If Laila's telling the honest truth right now, then all I can say is, *Hey, thanks for taking responsibility for all the crap my mom did.*"

Ignora, who had taken on the role of God among the angels in heaven, was Urushihara's mother. Gabriel was the first to reveal that to Chiho and the other visitors at Laila's Nerima apartment on that day. He also reminded them of the assorted nefarious deeds she did to the Sephirah children, as well as what she was doing to Ente Isla right now—but to Chiho the noncombatant, the first thought on her mind was how Urushihara was taking all this. Seeing him respond so nonchalantly to it all was, in its own way, even worse than if he took more drastic action.

"But if you want me to comment on all this as her son or whatever…hmm…"

Chiho perked up, hoping for something more substantial from him.

"…I guess I kinda resent her tossing me into the demon realms by myself? That, and not bothering to search for me afterward. But it's been fun with the demons, so… Like, I think it was a much better life then I woulda had up in heaven, where most people ain't much better than living zombies. It's not like I hate her so much I wanna act on it or whatever. I mean, it was a zillion years ago, so I seriously don't remember most of it."

"You don't even remember her at all?"

"Well, c'mon, do you remember every conversation you had with your friends or your mom in kindergarten or first grade or whatever?"

"No, but..."

"'Cause maybe I don't look it, but I've lived at least a few times longer than Maou has. And really, living in the demon realms has kinda kept me busy for most of that time. It's been superfun. So no, I'm not gonna remember my ancient history too much. To me, maybe Ignora's my mother by blood, but to put it in a way you'd get, it'd be like finding out your archnemesis is, like, your great-great-great-great-great-grandmother from three hundred years ago. It's all so way, way in the past, and we really oughta be thinking about now instead."

That wasn't something she really wanted to hear from Urushihara, whose life now mainly consisted of holing up in the closet and leeching off Maou's hard work, but it was clear that Urushihara had no sentimentality for Ignora.

"The past is the past, dude. Sometimes people get motivated by it, and sometimes they don't. In this case, I'm the leader of the side that doesn't, and Laila's the leader of the side that does."

"That kind of thing, huh?"

"Yeah. I dunno how much Laila and Gabriel told you, but judging by that look on your face, I guess a lot, right? The Cataclysm of the Devil Overlord and everything Ignora did and all that."

"Um... Pretty much."

It wasn't the kind of conversation one normally had over French fries at the MozzBurger in front of the rail station, but she did hear a lot.

"So yeah, it's really none of my business, and that means it's even less the business of someone like Ashiya or Maou, who wasn't even born yet. Maybe it's different for Emilia—I dunno if she's immortal now or not, but whatever. But honestly, I don't really see Maou saying yes to Laila. I mean, that's the whole reason why me and Ashiya are going around with demonic force in our pockets.

Y'know, just in case Laila does something stupid in an attempt to drive Maou into action."

"Really...?"

Chiho understood what Urushihara meant, but it was difficult for her to swallow. Why, though, she couldn't say.

"Plus," he added, picking up on this, "wouldn't that be better for you?"

"Huh?"

"You don't want him and Emilia to say yes, do you?"

"W-well, I...................................... No. You're right, I don't."

Several images projected themselves upon her brain during that pause. If she could believe everything Laila said, her desire to keep Maou and Emi on Earth was essentially the same thing as telling Ente Isla and everyone who lived on it to take a hike. The "good" Chiho inside her kept shouting about how she wouldn't allow that, but there was no point lying about her current feelings to Urushihara. Not being truthful right now, when he was being oddly frank with her for a change, would keep her from getting the answers she sought.

"I mean, all I really want is to keep Maou and everyone from leaving. Why would they even be willing to just abandon their lives and get involved with all that? That's kind of how I think about it."

"Yeah. I'm not exactly a fan, either. Like, why do we have to throw away this totally chill and stable environment just so we can go risk our lives somewhere far away?"

Chiho noted that Urushihara's stable lifestyle was being supported by the difficult sacrifices of many, many people around him. But now, of all moments, wasn't the time to sass back at him.

"I know that it's super-selfish of me," she said. "If that's what Maou and Yusa decide to do, I have no right to make them give that up. But Laila and Gabriel are just being way too arbitrary here."

"I totally agree. They're the ones who made this mess. They oughta clean it up."

Again, Urushihara was one to talk, but he was right. They couldn't clean up their own mess, so instead they were going on about the end of the world in an attempt to get Maou and Emi to do it. Chiho couldn't accept that. Hearing Gabriel talk about "the boss of us parasites" at MozzBurger the other day cleared the air on a lot of previously opaque mysteries, but that was all still just history. It didn't change what he and Laila wanted the demons to do for them.

Chiho hadn't seen Laila or Gabriel since that day, but looking at how Emi closed the gap between herself and Laila a little, it seemed like they were a step or two past the stalemate from before. Maou still hadn't made his intentions clear, though, and for Chiho, this December remained a month fraught with unease.

"Plus, you probably know more about this than I do, but Maou's gonna be pretty busy soon, yeah?"

"Oh, yeah, you're right."

Just as she recalled during Kaori's conversation, Chiho had a strong hunch about something that would keep Maou from accepting Laila's terms. Something that, if you knew Maou as intimately as she did, would be the first thing to cross your mind.

"And if *he's* busy, that's gonna affect Emilia substantially, and I haven't heard anything about Laila and her reconciling yet… By the standards of *your* life span, hey, no big rush, right?"

Hearing that said by Urushihara, who had lived several times as long as the centuries-old Maou, Chiho was oddly convinced. Certainly, if the Devil King made the choice Chiho and Urushihara assumed he would, it seemed like things on Earth could go along as usual for at least another two or three years. By that time, Chiho would be in college, enjoying far more freedom of choice and a better idea of where her emotions lay in all this.

"Like, this thing's exactly what Maou's been gunning for this whole time, right? I seriously doubt he's gonna throw it all in the garbage so he can skip out on this whole planet."

"I…I don't think so, either. And Yusa probably thinks the same thing."

Chiho took a notebook out of her bag and examined the MgRonald shift schedule written inside. Maou's shifts for today and the next several days had been crossed out and rewritten in a few spots.

"Yeah, he's been working at this for so long," she lovingly observed as her finger traced over what she wrote in the old shifts' place. The handwritten note read:

"Maou full-time training!!"

✳

Just as Chiho and Urushihara were chatting, Emi Yusa, rapidly approaching the seven PM end of her shift, raised a curious eyebrow at the figure walking through the automatic doors, likely the final customer of her workday.

"Hello! Come up to the counter when you're ready."

The customer needed no instruction, recognizing Emi the moment he went inside. He headed straight up to her.

"One Teriyaki Burger meal with large fries and a large hot coffee."

"All right."

She punched the order into the register, stated the price, accepted the customer's thousand-yen bill, and provided the change. A few more moments and his order was arranged on a tray and in his hands. Without another word, he took a seat, not even stealing a glance at her.

"That's uncommon."

Here was Shirou Ashiya, going to MgRonald during the dinner hour and eating a full meal. For him, this was highly unusual—eating out alone and upsizing his meal to boot. Plus, he was sitting on a barstool fiddling with his smartphone the entire time. It was so unlike the Ashiya she knew, she began to wonder if this was a nefarious angel posing as him.

"Saemi, aren't you going off?"

"Huh? Oh, yeah."

It was Akiko Ohki, one of the veteran part-timers, calling at her from behind. Emi looked up at the clock that was just a bit past seven now, removed her visor, and gave a sidelong glance at Ashiya as he continued pecking away at his phone.

"Hey, once I clock out, can I order dinner from you guys?"

"Oh, you want me to put it in as a crewmember meal now?"

"Sure thing. Umm, I'll get a Bacon Pepper Burger Set with a side salad and orange juice."

"Got it. Go ahead and get changed, and I'll have it waiting for ya."

"Thanks a lot."

Emi gave a light bow to Akiko and then went back to the staff break room. As she changed, she thought about Ashiya's potential motivations.

"He ought to know that the Devil King and Chiho aren't working today…but I guess he didn't have any business with me?"

Their eyes definitely met just now…but maybe it's because Emi just happened to be the only cashier on duty at the time. Either way, Ashiya couldn't have just come to MgRonald for dinner on a whim. He had a reason, and Emi didn't know what it could be.

Once back on the dining floor, Emi found Akiko waving at her. Paying for the crewmember meal—a 30 percent discount, essentially—she picked up the tray, pretended to search for a seat for a few moments, and then sat directly in front of Ashiya. The barstool seating at MgRonald featured a partition that ran across the long table, making sure that customers facing one another didn't have to deal with awkward stares, but he still had to know Emi was right there. But Ashiya, faintly visible through a gap between two partition panels, kept staring at his phone, slowly working through his fries. Emi, for her part, popped open the plastic case on her salad and began spearing the red leaf lettuce with her fork.

"What do you want?"

Ashiya spoke first. The restaurant was relatively empty, and it was only Emi and Ashiya at the bar seating, so they could hear each other well enough.

"What do *you* want?" she countered. She couldn't see Ashiya's expression through the panel, but then he couldn't see her. "Why are you at the Mag this time of night? Don't you have dinner to cook?"

"We are all eating separately tonight."

"Huh. Don't see that every day."

In fact, it was beyond shocking.

For Maou, at least, Emi could imagine him eating dinner out today easily enough. The schedule provided last month had him on shift right now, but following subsequent plans, he was away from the store today, along with manager Mayumi Kisaki. Takefumi Kawata and Akiko Ohki, the next most senior crewmembers after Maou, were both handling manager duties in his place—but there was no way Ashiya wouldn't be aware of his roommate's whereabouts.

"You're letting Lucifer do whatever?"

"I do not see how that involves you."

He had a point, but as someone who understood the financial situation at Devil's Castle, Emi was honestly worried. Plus, it simply wasn't like Ashiya to leave Urushihara unleashed like this.

"If someone I know starts acting totally uncharacteristic like this, I'm going to be worried about that, all right?"

"Oh-ho! So you think you have an iron grasp on everything involved in our lives?"

"Not everything but probably ninety percent, yeah. Enough that I know how weird this is for you."

"Do not interfere with customer privacy. You are on staff, are you not?"

"You know, whenever you try turning society's rules against me like that, for better or for worse, it's usually because you're doing something you don't want me or Bell to know about."

"…" Ashiya fell silent, seeming a little peeved behind the partition.

"Well, whatever." Emi stopped pushing him. "I dunno what's up with you, but yes, that was rude to you as a customer. I'm sorry."

"Mm…"

"Take your time. I'm leaving once I finish dinner."

"…"

The sounds of Emi finishing her meal continued but not for long. In a few minutes, she stood up and began to take her tray to the garbage.

"Yusa."

Ashiya's sudden voice stopped her.

"Have you seen Ms. Suzuki recently?"

"—!"

Emi gasped and turned around. Ashiya was still sitting on his barstool, back turned to her.

"...I haven't seen her in about two weeks. She did...text, but..."

"Ah. Good, then."

"What about her?"

Was there something too sharp in her voice? Emi regretted the question almost immediately. It totally revealed that she knew all about what was going on between them. Rika had asked her for advice the day before she had approached him; that smartphone of his was Rika's personal recommendation even—and Emi knew how it all turned out in the end.

What Emi didn't know was the whole process in between. All she knew was that she hadn't seen her in two weeks, and the text Riku had sent simply read, "It didn't work out. Thanks anyway for your help." Their lack of communication since was starting to create a cloud of anxiety for her—and now Ashiya was treating her question with silence. Should she take it to mean he was done with her?

All kinds of emotions were starting to form a voice in her mind. What happened to Rika? What did he do to her or say to her? If Emi could, she wanted to drag him out of the restaurant and make him lay out all of yesterday's events to her right this minute. But after a few short moments, Emi bottled it all up, turned her eyes away, and left.

"Oh, right, you're off now, Yusa?" Kawata asked at the exit, fresh from a delivery run. "Take care on the way home."

"Yeah. You, too."

She gave him a quick nod, not bothering to look back toward the demon at the counter.

Leaving the restaurant's heat, she was greeted by a cheek-tingling cold, the sun a lost memory today. It drove her forward, down the Koshu-Kaido road alone, so she could stop by Suzuno's place and pick up Alas Ramus.

The frigid air cooled her head enough to make her think that leaving without demanding a response from Ashiya was the right thing after all. She knew Rika had a thing for Ashiya—really, Ashiya was the only one who *didn't* know. Having Rika say "It didn't work out" must have meant just one thing.

Emi didn't feel it presumptuous to assume that, if Ashiya had pulled a Maou and asked for time (or even said yes to her), Rika would be right at her door again seeking advice. Besides, by the time Rika approached her, she had already drummed up enough drive to *maybe* confess her love to him and was just de facto asking Emi for permission. But Ashiya simply refused it all—and now that he had, there was nothing Emi could do or even should do.

"What…did I even want for her?"

She didn't want to see Rika hurt. But she doubted Ashiya could have ever made her happy or had any real desire to.

"Haaah…"

The white breath she sighed out, from a heart unable to come to terms with itself, seemed to draw an image of Chiho in her mind.

"This is so selfish of me…"

Was Emi fine with Chiho and Maou being an item but not Rika and Ashiya? She began to suspect that she knew all along Rika had no chance, and it sickened her. Maou was being ridiculously indecisive, and as Laila, Suzuno, and Ashiya all pointed out yesterday, he didn't have it in him to act totally heartless toward the girl who admired him. Meanwhile, Ashiya had shed a fair bit of his callousness toward the human race in general, but during his whole time on Earth, he had always stuck to his guns. He was a demon, and someday he would return to Ente Isla and help conquer it again.

If he had turned Rika down a little while ago, maybe Emi, despite their friendship, would've seen it as merely one less obstacle to taking that demon down. But now she had seen him, and Maou, and Urushihara as individual people. She was different now. The remaining traces of her old Hero's soul was asking what she was hung up about, but right now Emi Yusa knew this person named Ashiya had hurt Rika's feelings, and it enraged her.

"It's so selfish…"

It was. It was extremely selfish. This rage of hers wasn't appropriate, for someone who had gone on for so long about killing them and hoping they'd die soon. But the truth was two of her most valuable friends were in love with people from different worlds, different species.

Wincing at the disorganized noise that prevailed in her heart, Emi came across someone familiar at the intersection up ahead. "...In this cold?" she couldn't help but blurt out—a voice mixed with annoyance, resignation, and a slight tinge of happiness that not even she picked up on. Not joy exactly—nothing that lofty. Just pure, childlike happiness.

"Oh, um, hello, Emilia. Back from work?"

It was Laila. How long had she been standing here, shopping bag hanging from her wrist? Ever since that apartment visit, they had crossed paths here a few times, Laila choosing this spot on the way home to ambush her. Her motives were obvious. The gap was ever so slightly narrower between them now, and she wanted to close it further. But the clumsiness of the move, coupled with the outright hatred Emi felt for her not long ago, made the situation seem almost comedic.

She didn't take this path home every day. Sometimes she had a quick bite elsewhere with the crewmates she had become decent friends with. Sometimes she stopped by the store to shop for Alas Ramus or Suzuno or Nord, her father. If Laila wanted to see Emi, she could always just wait at Room 101 in Villa Rosa Sasazuka. She knew that.

"How many hours have you been standing here?"

"Huh? Oh, um, no, I was going to your father's place today, and I was just done shopping along the way, so..."

"Your nose. It's bright red. And that bag's from the supermarket across from Sasazuka Station."

"Oh...!" Laila instinctively brought a hand to her nose.

"You know you can just stay at Father's place if you're cold."

"N-no, but then I wouldn't be able to talk alone with you..."

Laila's motives made sense. She was a long-lost mother, struggling to find the right distance to take in this relationship. But the logic she chose made her sound like a stalker.

"...I'll take that."

"Huh? Ah!"

With a small sigh, Emi took Laila's shopping bag.

"That—that's pretty heavy, Emilia..."

"With as many shopping trips as I've done with Bell and Alciel, this is nothing."

Without waiting for a reply, Emi began walking home. Laila froze for a second but snapped out of it and began to give chase, walking side by side a slight distance away. Emi, sensing that Laila was trying to find something to say and failing, finally spoke up.

"So what? You didn't get your apartment all messy again, did you?"

"Huh?! N-no, no, it's totally clean! Um, still!"

"Oh, come on."

Emi smiled a little, then went back to her usual scowl. She couldn't give Laila an honest smile yet.

Previously, when she visited Laila's apartment to find out what kind of life she was living in Japan, she found the place so astoundingly cluttered and unkempt that a robot vacuum would take one look and trundle right out the door and off the walkway to its death. Emi had dived in first to start cleaning it up, and really just the cleanup took the entire day. The only talking the whole time was done by Laila and Nord. Emi and Laila, with no idea what to talk about, said almost nothing apart from when they bickered over what pile of strewn clutter should go where. Even this, however, was clear progress from how things were before—and now the gap was narrow enough that they were actually walking down the street together.

"Is work keeping you busy?"

"Well, every company's short-staffed during the holiday season. But unlike *you*, I'm not working against the clock to save millions or anything, so it's all good."

"Um... Oh. Well, good."

Emi didn't know what was "good" about that—it wasn't like she had said she wasn't busy—but this, at least, was an actual conversation. It continued along in fits and starts as they walked. When they reached Sasazuka Station, Emi suddenly stopped, looking at the intersection ahead and the Shuto Expressway overpass that hung above it.

"Emilia?"

She could recall Urushihara attacking this overpass, Chiho almost getting crushed under it, Maou and Ashiya transforming into demons, her fighting against her supposed friend Olba, and then Chiho's face at the end, still smiling despite knowing everything that had just happened.

"No, um, just a…"

I wasn't expecting any of this.

How many times in the past year-ish had she had that thought? If only she or Maou had just got on with it and erased Chiho's memory, neither of them would be standing here right now. But after defeating Urushihara, Maou had showed no sign of doing it. So Emi, recalling this as she stood there with Laila, decided to bet on a possibility that nobody who knew the Devil King Satan would dare imagine. It wasn't a bet she had ever discussed with Emeralda or Albert. Really, it was just something she had half-jokingly suggested to Maou before even making friends with Chiho. She didn't expect him to say yes, and he didn't, of course, but now Maou had everything he needed to make it happen. That's just how it seemed to her.

If Ashiya said no, what about Maou?

"Hey, Laila?"

"Yeees?"

"Why did you get married to Father?"

"Huhh?!" Laila practically jumped off the ground. "Wh-why? Where did *that* come from?! I just… I mean, if you love someone, you marry them, don't you?"

"…"

Something Emi had thought back when she asked her father how they came to know each other was that the way a husband or wife describes their partner had a far deeper, more profound impact on their children than either could ever imagine. Now that feeling was coming back.

"I'm not asking about that. You're a millennia-old angel, and my father's a human who won't even make it to a hundred. What made you want to get together with him?"

"Um…?"

"Because to you, the time you spend with him is nothing but a blip, isn't it?"

"…Oh, that's what this is about?"

"Sooner or later, you're going to be separated, and you're the one who's gonna have to see him go. So why…?"

"I wouldn't have joined him if I wasn't prepared for that."

Her voice was gentle as always but strong as well. It was rare, coming from her.

"And no, the time I spent with him in Sloane wasn't that long a part of my life, but it was one of the most fun, precious, and wonderful times I ever had."

"…So what made you choose Father?"

"Choose him?"

"He's a normal human being. He's not nobility, not the descendant of some great Hero. He couldn't contribute anything to the type of battles you're fighting. So why?"

This, in a way, was the biggest question Emi had about Nord and Laila's relationship. However, Laila's response to it was as simple as it was aggravating:

"Emilia, don't tell me you've never been in love before?"

"Whaaaaaat?!"

Not only was it not an answer at all, but it sounded like nothing less than taunting. It made Emi's face turn bright red, but her flying into a rage was nothing Laila hadn't seen before. Instead, she gave her daughter a worried look.

"E-Emilia, you're not the kind of woman who asks a man what his salary is before anything else, are you? Like, figuring out his job and promotion prospects so you can hit the jackpot when you get married? You're more about money and stability than feelings?"

"What—what—what're you talking about?! You're not making any sense!"

"What are *you* talking about? Because that's the only conclusion you're giving me. You know that isn't any good. Sure, it's one thing if the man you choose is violent or a gambling addict or something, but before anything else, love is about whether he makes your heart skip a beat or not!"

"Wait a minute! This isn't what we were discussing! I…!"

"You asked me why I married your father, didn't you? It's because I fell in love with him, of course. What more reason do I need?"

"That… What—what do you mean by *love*?! I'm not asking about that—"

"If you're asking about his bloodlines, or the Sephirah, or whether he can fight or not, I never thought about any of that. I just fell in love with Nord Justina. If you're looking for a reason, that's about all I've got."

"That's all…?"

"And I'm sure your father would say the same thing."

"He…"

She couldn't deny it. She had heard all the sweet words Nord had for her, alongside Emeralda and Suzuno. The fact her friends eavesdropped on their conversation made it all the more embarrassing.

"Of course, it was pretty tough at first when we decided to get married. To all the people in Sloane, I was just this strange girl who wandered in out of nowhere. Some of them accused me of being a swindler, trying to trick that man out of his house and fields after both his parents died. So I worked. I worked hard, and I learned about agriculture and animal husbandry and so on. I knew a thing or two about medicine, too, so I did things like help the village's midwife. So little by little, I worked myself into life in the village. And maybe we couldn't live like upper-class nobles, but working with him, traveling with him to the little cabin we had in the mountain, stargazing with him, playing in the river, reading the books his father left behind... We had all kinds of fun things to do."

To Laila, all this may have been just the other day. But as she focused on her nostalgia, it began to sound more and more like ancient history.

"Your father knew I was an angel from the start, thanks to the way we met each other. He knew he was going to die before me, but he stayed with me anyway. We talked things over, we argued, but we still stayed together. That's really all I can say about it."

"But..."

"And yes, it is sad," she said, verbalizing what Emi couldn't. "Your father's going to be an old man someday, and I'll see him off not looking much different from when I met him. I knew all that, but I couldn't help but fall in love with him. I told you, you need that heart-skipping moment!"

"Heart skipping... I mean..."

"It's hard to learn how to be kind or sincere. But he had that from the very start. That alone was more than enough to make me love him. I wanted our hearts to be together, no matter what it took. Is that enough of an answer?"

Was it? Emi could tell that a super-long-lived angel approached marriage with roughly the same mentality as any human being. But could that lead to happiness? She couldn't tell.

"Look, Emilia," Laila continued, reading her mind once more. "Maybe you won't like to hear it but let me just tell you this."

"Wh-what?"

"You can never tell if one moment or another's going to be truly happy for you until long after it's passed. Happy memories from the past can torture you in the present, if things aren't going so well any longer. But if you're so afraid of being hurt that you can't act any longer, you're never going to find happiness. If you don't make any moves, you'll keep sliding down the hill of unhappiness without realizing it, and little by little, it's going to cut you apart."

"..."

"Of course, sometimes action leads to unhappiness. Even injury. That's about all I can say about it, and I've lived for thousands of years. Would you call me unhappy?"

"That's not for me to decide," Emi replied.

"No. I'm the only one who can. Luckily, I find being married to your father to be a glorious thing, and I don't regret any of it. And I trust that he thinks so, too."

"Yeah, that much I can guarantee."

"Oh?"

"Nothing… I'm sorry if it sounded like a weird question."

"It's fine. Ask me more! Ask me anything."

"Don't get carried away. Father's waiting for us. Let's go back to the apartment."

Emi pushed her frustrated mother forward. It did nothing to dampen her drive.

"If you treat it as 'going back' to the apartment, why don't you just move in?"

"Eventually."

Emi stepped forward. She had talked too much, she thought, and now was the time to end the conversation. As far as she was concerned, she didn't have a care in the world for Laila and Gabriel's plans, and she could never let on otherwise. *That* was Emi's problem, well outside whatever distance she took with Laila.

"Oh, Emilia?"

"What?"

"I know I told you about my heart skipping a beat and everything, but don't let that happen to you over someone like *that*, all right?"

"Someone like who?"

She looked where Laila was pointing, then froze. The guy turned away from them… Was that Urushihara?

"I mean, it's partly my fault that Lucifer turned out like…that. But from what Satan, Alciel, and Chiho told me about his life in Japan, just… Not him."

"That's not funny…in ways you'd never even know. Seriously. And *this* isn't funny, either. Why's he going around with nobody guarding him?!"

"Ah, Emilia!"

The sight of Urushihara alone in public was enough to fill Emi with an indescribable urgency. She hurried after him, Laila trotting behind.

"Dude! First Bell, then Chiho Sasaki, and now you guys?! How many times longer you think I've even been living than you?! I'm seriously starting to get mad, yo!"

And all the way back to the apartment, the pair had to listen to him.

✳

It was a few hours after Emi and Laila returned to Villa Rosa Sasazuka, withstanding Urushihara's whining the whole way. The moment the dinner rush at the MgRonald by Hatagaya station subsided, a new kind of chaos burst onto the scene.

"The banquet has begun!"

This, it went without saying, was the archangel Sariel—aka Mitsuki Sarue, general manager at the Sentucky Fried Chicken in Hatagaya—and he was back to contribute to the bottom line of Kisaki's restaurant.

"Tonight, once more, the beating of my heart echoes higher than the bells tolling the holy night, feeding the flames of my love! Yes, tonight I, Mitsuki.................... Oh, she's not here again?"

""Good evening, sir!""

Lately, Sariel had developed some kind of extrasensory organ that told him within seconds whether Kisaki was at work or not. Before, whenever Sariel paid a visit, most of the crew would put on the most strained smiles possible and push Maou in his direction. Now that this charade had been going on for a good six months, they were mostly used to it, treating him like a regular customer with only a small amount of bewilderment.

The other customers, however, weren't having it. The so-called "one-man flash mob" was found at MgRonald for only around half an hour, always after the breakfast, lunch, and dinner peak times, so even a lot of the regulars didn't know him. To someone just passing through, the sight of him at full tilt could make them spill their drink all over their shoes.

And today, in fact, the tirade had just made someone drop their smartphone on the floor.

"O-oh, no..."

The hapless victim picked the phone up, checking it for any obvious damage. His voice and his behavior were familiar to Sariel.

"Hmm? Well, well! Here's a sight for sore eyes."

"..."

Recognizing him as the Great Demon General, Sariel crept up to him, a shocked look on his face. "You, eating alone at a time like this? To what do I owe this extraordinary sight, Al...um, no, uh, Ashiya, right?"

Not interacting with Maou and the gang on a regular basis, it took a moment for him to recall Ashiya's Japanese name.

"You really *do* carry on like that?" an exasperated Ashiya asked. "My liege had told me as much, but..."

"Carry on like what?"

"That... Well, the shouting about Ms. Kisaki all the time. And the love letters you read out loud."

"Love letters? How rude of you. I am simply giving vocal form to the surging passions that spill out from my heart in real time. If I prepared my statements in advance, they would lose their rawness, the strength to strike at your very heart."

It was hard to tell how serious he was being. If he meant every word of it, Ashiya certainly had to appreciate the vast vocabulary Sariel described his passions with.

"Regardless, neither Ms. Kisaki nor Maou is present today."

"I know. The sights, the sounds, the very scent in the air changes with her presence... Wait. Did I hear you right? Neither of them are working?"

"No."

"What is the meaning of that? Why are both of them gone? Isn't Maou a shift supervisor? Why is MgRonald running without a manager *or* a shift supervisor? Do they have someone regional on hand?"

"They do not. Maou and Ms. Kisaki are away from this location today so that Maou can begin his full-time employee training."

Ashiya, not having to face up to Sariel's bizarre behavior on a daily basis, had no idea how careless a statement this was. Sariel's face seemed to literally waste away, a deathly rage building within his eyes.

"Maou and Ms. Kisaki are…together?"

"W-wait a moment. What are you thinking? It is only for work purposes."

"Full-time employee training? And my goddess is accompanying the Devil King?"

"N-no… I am not sure you could call it 'accompanying,' no…"

"…Nnnnngh…"

A groan like the wail of a goblin from hell erupted from the bottom of Sariel's throat. He turned toward the front counter and marched up to it. It made Kawata visibly rear back as he tried his best to follow the book script.

"Um, welcome to Mg—"

"I must work here, too!!"

"—Ronal— Whaaat?!"

He couldn't help but stammer out his surprise.

"You're still hiring part-time, are you not? I want to apply. Sign me up for an interview. I'll have a résumé for you at once!"

"Ummmm, Mr. Sarue?! What are you, um, talking about?!"

"Kawata, are you really such a thickheaded moron that you fail to understand such a simple request?"

Being the world's most frequent visitor to the Hatagaya station MgRonald, of course Sariel knew the names of everybody on staff.

"All you have to do is tell your manager, Ms. Kisaki, that I, Sarue, applied for a part-time job at MgRonald. She will gladly contact me later for an interview."

"Uh, ummm, I, er, sorry? I mean, uh…"

Not even Kawata could react coherently to this. But asking him not to be flustered at the sight of the manager of a rival franchise applying for shift work would be too much for anyone.

"P-please, Mr. Sarue, calm down for a moment! I'll be sure to tell Ms. Kisaki that you stopped by!"

"You *always* tell her that I stopped by! Today I want you to tell her I'm applying for… Hngh?!"

"What is the meaning of this nonsense, you?"

Ashiya, no longer able to stomach the sight, stepped in to stop him.

"What are you…? Let go! I am deadly serious!"

"This goes beyond all common sense! Um, I will take care of this man for you. I apologize; would you be able to clean my table for me?"

"Oh, um, certainly, sir."

"Thank you. Come on."

"Let me go! Hands off me! What are you doing?! This has nothing to do with you!"

"I would be unable to face my liege if I told him I saw this and did nothing. This is exactly why I stayed on hand!"

Kawata just stood there, watching blankly as the notably tall man dragged out Sarue (no taller than Chiho) in a full nelson. Akiko Ohki, watching all this unfold from behind Kawata, gave him a compassionate pat on the black.

"Good job."

"Aki… What was that all about?"

"I dunno, but I guess this MgRonald's pretty screwed as long as Ms. Kisaki isn't around, huh? There's no telling what kind of people you run into in this world."

"Man. Maybe I shouldn't take over my family's restaurant after all. If I have to deal with this every night…"

"I don't think you'll see anyone quite like this, no…"

"Wow, though… Are December sales at the Sentucky in the tank or something?"

"Yeah, working full-time in this biz seems pretty stressful. Sometimes I wonder if I'm really up for it."

Neither Kawata nor Akiko took their eyes off the front door for a while after the mismatched pair left.

"Take your hands off me! Enough of this! I'm going to call for help!"

"You've attracted quite enough attention already, thank you. And if I see you running back in and continuing with that charade, I will make sure His Demonic Highness informs Ms. Kisaki."

"All right! All right! Just let me go!"

Even at half past ten in the evening, there were still plenty of people hanging around Hatagaya station, most of whom were now watching Ashiya whip Sariel around like a rag doll. Finally regaining his composure, Sariel gave him a hateful glare once he was finally put down, but he simply fixed his clothing, making no sign of running.

"Ah, what have I done? I suppose the blood must have gone to my head."

"Did you have any in there beforehand?"

"Pfft. Stupid Devil King. Full-time employee training? The thought of him alone with Ms. Kisaki... How repulsive! I knew the Devil King had an obsession about becoming a salaried employee, but was he angling for my goddess this whole time?"

"Hold it. I will *not* allow you to engage in wild speculation about my liege. And why do you think they will be alone at all?"

"What are you talking about?" Sariel snorted. "At times like these, companies have never been more reluctant to bring on more full-time salaried employees. If we are talking about promoting from the hourly ranks, then being invited to training would be unthinkable without the recommendation of a manager. With Sentucky, at least your direct supervisor becomes your training partner, teaching you everything you need to know... Yes, everything... Curse youuuu, Devil King!!!!"

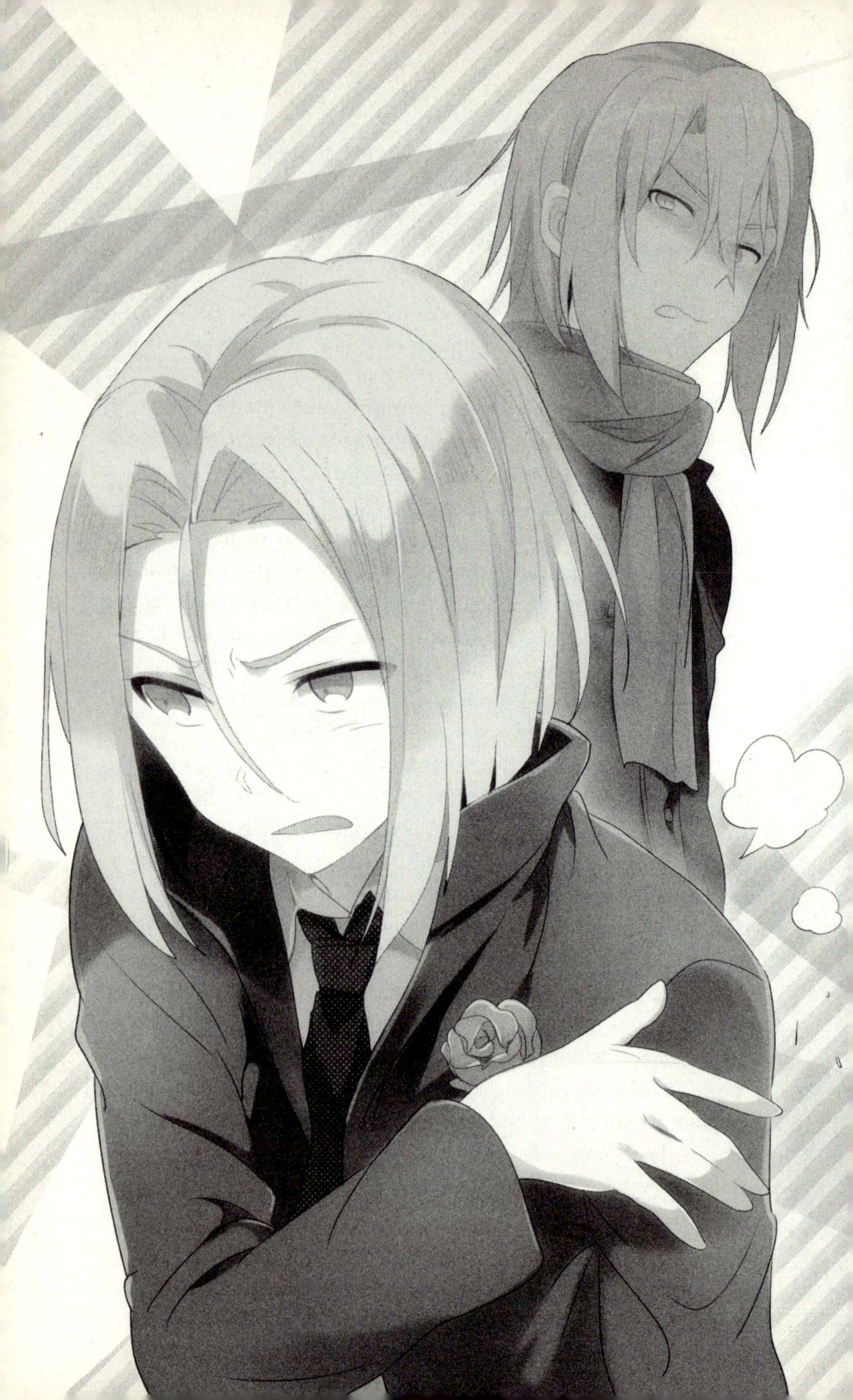

Sariel had succeeded mainly in making himself angry, but given his status as a full-time SFC manager, his words held some weight. Still, as the Devil King's right-hand man, Ashiya couldn't take this sitting down.

"A word of advice. No matter how you slice it, His Demonic Highness and Ms. Kisaki are not engaged in the kind of liaison you are imagining."

"And how would you know?!" the archangel countered, shooting the Great Demon General down. "We're talking about a man and a woman! You can never predict what kind of infinitesimally small seed could sprout the seedlings of love! The Devil King is Ms. Kisaki's most trusted of employees, someone trustworthy enough to reveal her own career dreams to! Someone she has worked with on the front lines over thick and thin! Nothing could possibly make me more anxious!"

"You—you truly believe so?" Ashiya was a little surprised. Sariel seemed to be worried for far more realistic reasons than he had surmised. Based on what everyone from Maou himself to Chiho, Emi, and Suzuno had let on about, he figured the archangel would have some different, more insane concern.

"I had wanted to ask you, actually..."

"What?!" Sariel snapped back.

"What kind of relationship do you even want to build with Ms. Kisaki?"

"Hmm." Something changed in Sariel's eyes. "A thorny question."

"Oh?"

"Considering both of our lives, it would likely be best for both of us if I took on the Kisaki name, rather than the other way around."

"...Oh?"

"Plus, I may be a fool in love, but I am not optimistic enough to believe Ms. Kisaki sees me as marriage material right now. Currently, the issue is not whether she would be my wife but rather whether she's interested in me being her husband."

"........Um. One moment."

"What?"

"You are working on insane assumptions."

"What's so insane about that? I wouldn't act like that around her if I didn't have marriage in my sights."

"You have marriage in your sights, and yet you act like this?!"

"I know of no other way."

Ashiya could no longer hide his dumbfounded shock. "Er... No, um, that is to say, your approach is not the issue, perhaps. More to the point, you see a human being as a potential marriage partner?"

"What's so strange about that?"

When it came to Sariel, it had to be said, pretty much everything. But there was no point dwelling on that.

"You angels live hundreds of times longer than any human ever could."

"Yes. And? Do you think we could never be happy because of our life spans? Is that what you are insinuating?" He shrugged. "What I'm trying to say," he continued before waiting for an answer, "is that it's up to *me* to decide whether I'm happy or not, do you see? Could love truly be called love if a few passing words from someone else was enough to make it waver?"

"Or could you call it love if it is as completely one-sided as it is with you?"

Even with having this pointed out, Sariel just stared at Ashiya and chuckled. "I heard you were a strategic genius on the battlefield. Who knew you found it difficult to grasp concepts as simple as this?"

"What?"

"I'm the only one who decides whether living with Ms. Kisaki is a happy thing for me or not."

"Wh-what?"

"But would Ms. Kisaki be happy living with me? I could spend my whole life never knowing the answer to that."

"W-wait, what are you...?"

"I'm saying, only you have the ability to feel whether you're happy. Happiness, of course, requires effort on your partner's part as well—but would my partner see my efforts as a happy thing? The answer to that lies strictly within the heart of Ms. Kisaki. I am not her, you see, so even with my eternal angelic life, I could never truly feel her inherent happiness the way she feels it."

This caught Ashiya completely off guard. He lost his voice for a moment. In one way, Sariel's statement could be construed to mean "all that matters is me and screw what anyone else feels," but examine the actual words, and he meant the exact opposite.

"You've been alive for, what, a thousand years? Hardly a short life. But have you ever exhibited such absolute happiness that nobody would ever doubt for all time that you were happy? With all my experience in life, I can confirm to you that you haven't. Thus, to me, happiness is making a continual effort toward that absolute happiness, something I can hardly say exists for me. Right now, though, I am closer to that kind of happiness than I've ever been before in my life. Physically speaking, no less!"

He defiantly pointed back at the MgRonald, still visible in the distance.

"And fortunately for me, I have an example right here."

"An example? You mean…"

Sariel nodded. "Exactly! Emilia's mere existence is proof positive of a happiness forged across races, across worlds! When word of her went around the heavens—oh, heads *rolled*, believe you me! And now I firmly believe that furor was a shot to my heart, a clarion call to shed the malaise of ten thousand years and finally seize the initiative with the goddess I have encountered here!"

Both arms were now raised high as Sariel kept shouting, pedestrians keeping their distance as they walked past. Ashiya remained still, as if strapped to the ground.

"And I believe you have heard too, no, Alciel? About Gabriel's plan?"

"…You…"

"Because I certainly didn't—not until fairly recently. If I had known, I would have banished him and Raguel from the heavens centuries ago! That was well before I was aware fate had implanted a goddess into the living world by the name of Mayumi Kisaki, after all. I believed the guidance of the beautiful Ignora was what we needed to keep heaven alive…but no longer."

Sariel finally lowered his arms, running a hand down his long hair.

"If you have the earth under you, the sky above, the sea ahead, and your own freedom to enjoy, you can go anywhere. Now I've finally realized that the only thing stopping me is myself. Ignora, you see, tilts at utopias. If she ever caught sight of Earth or Japan, she would call it a confused, immature jumble of a world. But compared to life in a spotless, oppressive, white-walled room, I'll take this jumble any day, for it has so many colors to show that I've never seen! …Although I'll take a hospital nurse in a prim white uniform, too."

If it weren't for that final sentence, it would have been a fairly intelligent statement to make. But no. Just Sariel being Sariel.

"Why are you getting involved with other people *here*?"

And the unluckiness of having Mayumi Kisaki in business attire walk right up to him at this moment was also, well, pretty Sariel-like. He swiveled his head toward her, resulting in a fairly awkward body position to be frozen in.

"Oh…um, well, hello, Ms. Kisaki."

She was carrying a shoulder bag so full of documents that she couldn't close it all the way, a bag Ashiya recalled seeing before. The stylish peacoat framed her as an elite businesswoman, and it added even more force to her eyes as they shot a gaze at Sariel.

"Why are you revealing your nurse fetishes in the middle of the sidewalk?"

"N-no, um, we were having a philosophical conversation about what happiness truly means for a man…"

"Um, not exactly, you see, er…"

Sariel's quivering knees made Ashiya worry he could collapse at any moment. He wasn't lying, but even Ashiya was nervously stammering, not wanting to raise the ire of Maou's boss.

"Ah, hello again, Mr. Ashiya. I'm sorry you have to deal with the menace of our shopping center."

"Oh, no, um, I really was speaking with Mr. Sarue, so…"

"There's no need to defend him. Has this man been bothering you? I'll be happy to contact the mall administrator or the police if need be."

"No, it's fine! Nothing happened! Um, but weren't you working with Maou today, ma'am?!"

"Oh? Ah. You here to pick him up?" Kisaki accepted Ashiya's brute-force change of subject, still casting a suspicious eye on Sariel. "Well, sorry to disappoint, but we just split up at the rail station. I think he's headed home now. Oh, and I forgot to mention it to him, but could you tell him to buy a new pen case? 'Cause he's got this cheap plastic one with a hole in it, and he's gotta leave a better impression than that during training."

"C-certainly. I will tell him."

"Thank you… So, Sarue, can I borrow you for a sec? There's something else I want to ask you."

"Of course! Anything you like!"

Sariel, frozen in time until a moment ago, immediately brightened up like a dog wagging its tail, even though he had to recognize the bed of thorns awaiting him.

"Excuse me, then…"

Seeing that Kisaki's attention was on the errant angel, Ashiya took the opportunity to bow and walk briskly away. Sariel's shout stopped him.

"Oh! Ashiya! Tell your roommates that our promise from the other day's still active, so choose whatever life you want for yourselves!"

"Huh? …Ah. Uhh…"

He raised an eyebrow, unable to respond to this in front of Kisaki.

"And *you* stop giving people life advice! The one you're leading's gonna go straight to the gutter!"

Kisaki gave Sariel a whap to the back of the head. He looked almost elated about it.

Ashiya had planned to stay at MgRonald until closing time if he needed to, but with this new information, there was no need to stick around. Really, he was here mainly to keep watch over Maou's regular haunts—this MgRonald location in particular—just in case some foe, whether they existed or not, decided to target it.

"If His Demonic Highness was coming home," he muttered to himself once Kisaki and Sariel were too far away to hear, "he could have at least texted me so I could prepare dinner for him... Oh."

He was stopped by the display on his smartphone. One message was waiting.

"..."

It had arrived fifteen minutes ago, a simple message from Maou stating that he'd be home soon. It made Ashiya lower his eyebrows.

"Great. I must not have noticed the vibration with all of Sariel's carrying on. I think there was a way to change the vibration pattern on this...?"

He stopped on the sidewalk, staring at the screen for a while.

"..."

Then, as he stood there with a look of utter confusion on his face, the screen turned off and went back to lock mode.

"And a way to extend the standby time as well..."

But he didn't act on his needs, simply putting the phone back in his pocket. Somewhere, in that dark screen, he felt like he could see the bright-eyed face of that woman again.

"What am I even thinking...?"

Rika Suzuki had made no contact with him since that evening. But her phone book entry was still top among the dozen or so he had on this phone, and every time he saw the name, he could sense feelings lurking in his heart like none he had felt before.

"...I must hurry. My liege is already home."

Stuffing his numb hands in his pockets, Ashiya began loping on home. But the whole time it was an anxious walk back. Somehow, he couldn't shake the feeling that Sariel's words were looming right behind him.

◇

It was a few weeks ago, that day when Emi and Laila had grown just that little smidgen closer. The day Gabriel's question had been lobbed at Chiho and the others, just after they had left the archangel's dismal apartment:

"Have you guys ever heard of Nauru?"

Back then, his question had been just a little hard to appraise.

Nobody thought they had, although since this was Gabriel asking, Chiho assumed it was something to do with heaven or Ente Isla.

"Chiho Sasaki, maybe? Have you?"

For some reason, he was targeting the only Earthling in the crowd.

"Huh? Um, me?"

"Yeah. Or y'know, if anybody here would, it'd be you, mm-kay?"

"Oh, is this someone on Earth, maaaybe?"

Gabriel nodded at Emeralda.

"And not the paaarasite found in lakes and marshes in the northeastern section of the Northern Islaaand? The one where if a cow drinks from infested waaaters, it'll grow and proliferate so much that it'll literally eat the poor beast from the insiiide?"

Gabriel groaned at the woman. "Eww, no! Nothing that scary! What's wrong with you?!"

But as the rest of the table wondered whether such a creature actually existed or not, he revealed the answer:

"Anyway, Nauru's the name of an Earth nation. It's on an island in the Pacific Ocean near the equator, the third-smallest country in the world after Vatican City and Monaco. It's considered to be part of Micronesia, but it's, like, way the hell out from the rest of those islands. There aren't a lot of folks on it, either, so it relies on Australia for defense and currency and stuff. Japan had an airbase on it during World War II even."

The more he spoke, the more it sounded like somewhere on Earth after all. Chiho still had no idea about it, but based on what Gabriel hinted at, it was easy enough to imagine a nice little tropical getaway. But what did Nauru have to do with heaven?

"At one point in the twentieth century," Gabriel continued as Chiho sat with her own questions, "you could've called this place a literal heaven on earth. For one, nobody on the island paid any taxes."

"Oh?" Chiho blurted out, Suzuno and Emeralda looking just as surprised.

"In fact, every native Nauruan was given a basic income to live off of. Every man, woman, and child on the island received enough of a stipend from the government to handle all their basic needs. I'm not just talking about pensions Japan pays out to its old people—like, you'd make more money just going on welfare instead, mm-kay? I'm talking about everyone from age one to one hundred getting enough cash that they could eat out three times a day, replace their car with a new one each year, and still have enough left to screw around with. All that, without even working. And like I said, none of it was taxed."

"Wow, really?"

It was a life beyond anything Chiho could comprehend, but Gabriel gave her an emphatic nod. "Yeah! And anyone would react like that, huh? But it's true, mm-kay? Not a lot of people have Nauruan citizenship, but back in the day, the per capita income over there was way past Japan or the U.S. It was the highest in the world. I mean, nobody was throwing bags of money around or whatever, but in terms of world standards, everybody on that island was filthy rich."

Chiho just sat there, mouth open, as if hearing about an alien landscape. She couldn't say why Gabriel, an angel from another world, cared so much about a nation that was pretty minor by Japanese standards, but the initial shock far outweighed that concern.

"They...*were*?"

"Yeah."

"...What about now?"

Gabriel beamed, waiting for just this moment. "The unemployment rate's over ninety percent. One of the poorest nations in the world. They're managin' to keep it together mostly with international support."

"Uh, how'd *that* happen?"

Someone with a grasp of economics and politics as weak as Chiho's couldn't imagine what led to this. But someone with an understanding as strong as Emeralda's could.

"Did that nation have some kind of natural reeesource the rest of the world waaanted? And it's all been miiined now, so there you go?"

"Exactly. In particular, they had a lot of this mineral called phosphate."

Phosphate is an indispensable raw material in the industrial and agricultural fields. Since it is, it's in demand across the world. And Nauru had some of the world's best phosphate deposits formed by the droppings of birds accumulated over tens of thousands of years. The world's superpowers pushed into the island in the early twentieth century, seeking this phosphate, and the ruling government changed in and out, depending on who among them was on the rise. But after the war, when it joined the Commonwealth and became independent, the most striking thing was how the paradise Gabriel described was basically nonexistent by the nineties.

"So in just over ten years, it went from a paradise to this nation deep in poverty. It used to have some of the world's most valuable natural resources, but"—he snapped his fingers—"ten years. Which, hell, that's what you get for takin' something built over millennia and running through it in less than a century. Humans are a scary bunch, yeah?"

He was grabbing for another fry as he said this, only to be met with the empty bottom of the bag he was holding. He rolled his eyes.

"But there wasn't much they could do to avoid it. Once the phosphate was gone, all the international companies and laborers were bound to go with it. Nauru got poorer and poorer, and naturally they couldn't keep that basic income thing going. No money, no way to buy food. Now, Chiho Sasaki, what would you do if you were there?"

Chiho thought Gabriel was starting to sound like a history teacher, but she tried to use her unpolished intellect to cobble together an answer.

"Well, I'd look for work, but… I guess there wouldn't be any, huh? Like in the Great Depression. So I guess I'd try to farm or fish what I needed or go find a job in another country…"

Chiho's mind flashed back to the black-and-white photos of breadlines in her textbooks.

"Very good! If it was a *certain* freeloader I know, he'd probably just give up and starve to death right there."

Nobody needed to ask who Gabriel meant.

"That's the proper way to think about it. Nobody wants to starve. If you're starting to look short on cash, you search for work or try not to spend as much, right? That's normal." He flashed a self-effacing smile. "But guess what? Most Nauruans didn't do a thing."

"Huh?"

"It's not that they couldn't do anything. They chose to do nothing. Unless their families had already been living off the land for generations, most of them just sat there and watched their nation's industry and economy collapse."

"They didn't do anything? But that's just…"

"You gotta work if you wanna eat, as they say, mm-kay? And we only have that little adage because the people who lived before y'all really *did* work to eat."

This attracted the attention of Amane, who had spent the dinner mostly picking on Acieth and Erone, even as she worried about how quickly they were vacuuming up the contents of her wallet.

"The people of Nauru went too long without having to work," she explained. "During the phosphate glory days, most of the mining work was done by foreign labor, and before that, the locals either fished or traded or used what little arable land there was to farm. There wasn't even a currency-based economy in place. No matter which generation you look at, there was never this custom of laboring for money."

And even that fishing was just on a subsistence level. None of it was large-scale enough to develop into an industry. And the phosphate mining had plugged the island so full of holes right up to people's backyards that they couldn't even keep themselves fed any

longer. But despite that, the people of Nauru, which had spent generations living without working, never really accepted the premise
of labor for money.

This, of course, doesn't apply to every islander. Even now, Nauru is
home to trade and communication and industry and everything else.
It has the feature set needed to become a tourist destination if it wanted
to, and there are even efforts to find new veins of phosphate to prop up
that dying business. Some foreign-educated politicians are even trying
to use real estate and finance to revitalize the economy. With Nauru
being a generally laid-back place, the collapse of the economy brought
about no rioting or other major unrest; the already-small population
didn't suddenly shrink.

The people's determined disinterest in working, however, remains
a tough nut to crack. A combination of their eating habits during the
good old days and a Pacific Islander tendency to equate extra weight
with wealth has led to some of the world's highest rates of obesity
and diabetes. Most economic policies so far have failed, not stopping the decline and even accelerating it at times. Eventually it got
to the point where it accepted war refugees in exchange for aid, and
even the refugees turned their backs to them, saying they "couldn't
be here." The century-long dream of paradise was over, and it would
take an incomprehensibly long time to go back to a more traditional,
tranquil South Sea Island nation.

Chiho couldn't hide her surprise over such a nation actually existing. But she still didn't see how any of this connected to heaven.

"Now, y'know, it's not like I went over there to see it for myself.
This was just some of the stuff I found online back when I was holed
up in that Internet café, right?"

This didn't quite answer it. Chiho didn't think Gabriel brought
this up just so he could talk about this cool site on the Net he found.
But then Gabriel's face took an unexpected turn for the serious.

"So, um, how to put it? I guess you could say heaven right now's
kinda where Nauru was just before it started declining, 'kay? Most
of the angels don't want for a single thing up there, but me, Ignora,
the guardian angels... All right, the 'upper class,' if you insist on me

putting it that way… We all know that we can't expect the dream to go on forever, y'know? But nobody's tryin' to change anything, and nobody's even thinking about it."

He shifted his eyes from Chiho to Suzuno.

"Lemme ask ya. What's, like, the ultimate goal of you guys over in the Church? When you pray to God 'n' stuff, what are you expecting back?"

"Divine salvation and guidance to an eternal paradise, free of pain," replied Suzuno, who still acknowledged herself as a Church cleric. "That is the brunt of it. This assumes, of course, that this world exists and is reachable if you try hard enough. The paradise our scripture describes is one that can only be realized through the joint efforts of us all—such is the current mainstream interpretation in Sankt Ignoreido."

"All righty. So if an eternal paradise free of pain really did exist, what do you think people would do?"

"…Hmm."

Suzuno brought a hand to her chin, thinking about it for a moment, but the question seemed to give her little trouble.

"Then we would all descend into sin, or our emotional and ethical standards would tumble downward. Either way, human society as we know it would be toppled."

"Correct!" Gabriel gave this his very best golf clap, as Amane nodded her agreement. "Well, Ignora went and actually built that paradise. And she's still ruling over it now."

"Whatever do you mean by thaaat?" Emeralda asked.

"Humans," he replied, making an uncharacteristically serious effort in his word choice, "cease being human when they can't die. Or at least can't die unless they really, really try to. They just turn into this living…thing."

He used his right hand to make a throat-slitting gesture over his neck.

"Angels are basically immortal, but all that means is you don't die *naturally*, mm-kay? If your head explodes or you lose more blood than your body can replenish itself with, then you'll die all the same. But y'know, even if your heart gets all smashed up, as long as you got enough holy force to heal the wound, it's possible to revive you. That's one of the core tenets of holy magic, am I right? And yeah, maybe you'll have some aftereffects or whatever, but we all got a really good chance of surviving something that'd kill a normal human. And the amount of holy force we got connects directly to our immune system. I dunno the, like, science behind it, but we pretty much never get sick. Not even a sniffle."

"Ah, yes, I've heard about that."

Chiho recalled the impromptu magic seminar Suzuno had given her in the bathhouse before learning how to send an Idea Link. They nodded at each other.

"Yeah. Now, if you look at it the other way, with all the holy force we got, the passage of time can't do a damn thing to kill us. We can swear off food and water for thousands of years, but nothing related to metabolism or growth or illness will do us in. And what's what heaven is right now—a totally safe shelter, not a care in the world for humans, to be in a place where they can't die unless someone actively tries to kill them."

Not having to lift a finger to keep on living. In a way, just like Nauru of the day, where simply existing granted you enough money to live as long as you wanted.

"So thanks to that, the people in my homeland… Well, they kinda fell apart, you get me? It used to be a real community, full of real, mortal people—lots of different families and stuff—just like anyplace you'd see on Earth or Ente Isla. But thanks to a lot of coincidence and tragedy, plus all of Ignora's power, we got to be called angels. We weren't people any longer. After all, why would we be? We had no active goals left in life. We became immortal, and then too much time passed where we didn't have to do anything…and now we've forgotten what it means to have a goal."

In other words, the heavens, or the people of Gabriel's homeland, were like the Nauruans—sent money for free across multiple generations.

"Lemme remind you guys—how many angels have appeared before you so far?"

"Ummm…" Chiho glanced at Suzuno again as she counted on her fingers. "Sariel, Gabriel, Laila…"

"Raguel, Camael, the Heavenly Regiment… Would Emilia and Lucifer count, too?"

"Not too many, huh? We're supposed to be these crazy intelligent aliens steering the history of Ente Isla from behind the scenes, and we got, like, no one practically. Try to think about how many working demons there were when the Devil King invaded Ente Isla by comparison for me."

"When we carried out our sweep up of the Central Continent," Suzuno articulated slowly as she looked at Maou from the side, "we estimated their force to be at least fifty thousand."

Maou didn't offer any special reaction to this, but he didn't deny it, so it had to be a close estimation. It meant that probably several times that number of demons were slain by the Ente Islans, but while Maou took responsibility for that, Suzuno knew he didn't fault the enemy for it.

But now that everyone knew that statistic, Gabriel offered an even more surprising one of his own.

"Well, you know, the entire population of heaven is, maybe, a little over five thousand, you feel me? And over nine out of ten don't do jack with their lives. They just exist. They don't even try to do anything else."

"Just…five thousand?" Chiho croaked.

For the population of an entire species that had its own fully constructed society, that sounded outlandishly low. Gabriel nodded at her.

"My planet's a lot more scientifically advanced than Earth, and it's more magically advanced than Ente Isla, too. But the whole reason we're going around as angels on Ente Isla is 'cause the whole dang planet was ruined."

Gabriel casually tossing out the word *ruined* made Chiho, Suzuno, and Emeralda freeze. After all, it was Laila who was asking Maou and Emi to help with the crisis on Ente Isla.

"It's really the result of one tragedy on top of another." Gabriel sighed as he rested his head on a hand. "Right when the star at the center of our system was having a lull in its solar activity, there was this huge supernova in the next galaxy over. That itself wasn't a huge biggie; it was kind of like going without phone service for a day or two. That wasn't the issue. You can call it, like, a change in the air-flow of space—the pressure from the supernova just hit our entire planet dead-on from out of nowhere, and it brought a lot of harmful crap along with it. By Earth standards, I guess our star was in a pretty inactive period for, what, thirty years? So you didn't see any solar winds going around the stars that protected our planet, and then all of a sudden, this supernova sends a shock wave that carries all the crap in the local space right over to us. And *then*, just when our star gets active again, it started sending all that harmful matter back across the whole system. I tell you, it went from bad to worse to even worse. Of course, Ignora's scientists didn't figure all this out until long after it was too late."

"Weren't you one of those scientists, Gabe?"

Gabriel shook his head at Amane. "Nah," he replied as he gave another airy grin, "I was hardly into science, or medicine, or astron-omy, or whatever back then, sweets. When I was living on my home planet, I was chief of security at the research lab Ignora headed. The pay was, well, not exactly what the researchers got, but we all got along pretty well. I even knew a lot of the higher-ups... Man, I don't even remember the last time I talked about that place. Here I thought I'd forgotten most of it..."

He looked out at the window, a nostalgic tinge to his eyes as he watched passersby make their way across Nerima Station.

"But anyway, thanks to that wave of harmful particles, the whole planet got caught up in this huge, lethal pandemic. A few of the less powerful nations died out entirely. Ignora's lab was set up by top sci-entists from around the world to find an effective solution against this disease. It was actually set up in one of our moon colonies—we already had a long history in space, so it was to the point where, man, we were sending people to live on all kindsa planets around our local system. So here you had this Institute set up to protect mankind from this harmful matter and the pandemic—all its medicine, its astronomy, its holy magic, its climate, its geology, its civic policy, its architecture, its genetic engineering, and all the laws and economic policy and logistics that harnessed all that stuff. But then…"

Gabriel turned toward Acieth and Erone, currently fighting over Maou for control of his wallet so they could make another food order.

"Then well, we failed. We couldn't save the planet or anyone on it. In the space of less than twenty years, the pandemic wiped out every piece of our civilization. Our homeland. Someplace way more advanced than Earth, and I'm sorry, but way, *way* more advanced than Ente Isla. And that happened after war broke out worldwide over the immortality formula Ignora came up with. It's not even funny, is it? I couldn't believe how stupid we all were. It really freaked me out back then."

"In the midst of seeking paradise, you lost sight of your own standards?"

"Y'know, Crestia Bell, I'd like to say it was as noble as all that, but I'd be very much lying." Gabriel laughed at the question. "People were just too impatient, y'know? All they wanted was some magic that could sweep away this disaster as quickly as it appeared. Like, normally, you'd have to spend decades developing an antibody for the disease, or build secret underground shelter cities worldwide to evacuate to, or—hell—spend a century or so making this force field or whatever that blocked out the harmful radiation. But Ignora's talents refused to let her settle for that. She zoomed right past all that boring antibody junk and just found a magic formula for immortality instead. Everyone swarmed on it, of course. Like, who gives a flip about anything else? I'm lookin' out for numero uno, so gimme that body and I'll never have to worry about disease again! That's what I thought, y'know, and so did everyone else in the world. It wasn't a breakdown in standards—we all just exploded 'cause we couldn't hold out anymore, you get me?"

"So can I ask you something?"

"What is it, Amane?"

"How did you achieve immortality anyway?"

Her voice was stern, deep, as if she already knew the answer. Picking up on this, Gabriel turned his eyes toward Acieth, who had successfully relieved Maou of his wallet and was already racing for the cash registers.

"Ignora managed to find the last remaining traces of the Tree of Life on our planet. She found the Sephirah children who blundered their way into the human world."

THE DEVIL KING IS OUT OF THE OFFICE (2)

The following evening after Ashiya's boundlessly frustrating encounter with Sariel, a pair of young women stood in the middle of Shinjuku, surrounded by flashy Christmas signs but looking seriously miffed.

"Haaaaaaaaah…"

In the midst of this dazzling display of light and color, as Tokyo's retailers fell over themselves to make Christmas a shopping extravaganza for young and old alike, this pair acted like the bright lights were just too much for them.

"I feel so miiiserable…"

"I-is there any need to feel quite so downtrodden about it?"

They were grown women, actually, although they still looked youthful enough to be called young women. One wore a beret and drawled out her vowels; the other had her hair done up as tightly as her machinelike pronunciation.

"This is hardly the last time you will be here. There will be another occasion…"

"You know it won't be that eeeasy. That's what I'm so dowwwn about! Ugh…"

Emeralda Etuva sullenly eyed a Christmas tree on the other side of a store window. In her hand was a gelato cone, something she waited in line for despite how cold it was outside.

"Things are starting to look like so much fuuun, and now I have to go? I can't belieeeve it..."

Suzuno Kamazuki gave an awkward chuckle, one finger scratching at her cheek.

Only two days ago Emeralda received a rather angrily worded summons to return to her post. It was, of course, from Albert, whom Emeralda had left Western Island matters with on Ente Isla. As he put it: "I can't take any more of this. Get yourself back here already. Otherwise, we'll be so broke, we'll need a hundred times the budget for next year, and I'll have Rumack redo the entire Institute in her image before you can do anything about it."

Emeralda was supposed to be here on Earth just long enough to inform Emi about the trial proceedings against Olba, the man who threw all of Ente Isla into chaos. But before she could return, Laila showed up, Erone and the other Sephirah started acting out, this and that happened, and before she knew it, Emeralda had spent over a month away from home.

She had remained in constant contact with Albert, of course. He had taken pains to cover for Emeralda's absence, out of an abundance of concern for Emi's situation. But—perhaps noticing how Emeralda's trip was now less business and more pleasure cruise, or perhaps Albert really couldn't do the job of two people any longer—their Idea Links had grown testier as of late. Then, the day before yesterday, the gavel came down.

"Ahhhh, I wish I could've had some Christmas caaake... Or some roast turrrkey, at least..."

"Then why not enjoy that for lunch today? I am sure we can find a restaurant nearby offering that much right now."

But after getting so worked up about Christmas, New Year's, and all the traditions associated with the holiday period in Japan, Emeralda was now pouting like a spoiled child. A job, however, was a job, and she owed both Albert and General Hazel Rumack for allowing her to be gone from Saint Aile for so long. Emi, alas, couldn't get out of work today, so it was up to Suzuno to guide Emeralda around.

"Oh, but that's only good when you eat it the day you're meeeant to. Cheating and having it earrrrly isn't riiight."

"It isn't?"

Considering how unrecognizable and far removed Japan's Christmas food offerings were from the original intent of the holiday, the date on the calendar didn't seem to matter in Suzuno's eyes. But Emeralda was adamant. "Thiiink about it," she said, wagging her finger. "No matter how great it taaastes, you can't have that…um, *ozoni*, you call it? The rice and vegetable soup thing. It's *toootally* New Year's food."

"Um. Well, if you say so, perhaps."

Emeralda was already thinking ahead to the next holiday. Suzuno was disinterested. She had yet to experience a Japan-style New Year herself, and it wasn't like Emeralda would know more about one than her, so she fairly well doubted the validity of her protests.

"Ohhh, but doesn't *ozoni* make it sound like a French or Itaaalian dish? Like, 'Oooh, waiter, I'll have a piiizza margheriiita *ozooooni*, please'?"

"Ah, I have actually heard about experiments along those lines— using French or Italian ingredients to make an *ozoni*-type soup. I will stick with tradition myself. Mochi rice balls, vegetables, clear soup stock, and all is well."

"…Waaaay to miss the joooke, Bell."

"Huh?!"

Being criticized by Emeralda came as a bolt out of the blue to her.

"But no point complaaaining about it, I suppose. Time to pick up some souvenirs and prepare for the jourrrney."

"Er, yes…"

Suzuno still didn't get the joke—if there ever was one—but regardless, their first stop was the main concourse of Shinjuku Station, where Emeralda quickly whipped out a handwritten shopping list and began marking out her stops. Suzuno took a peek at the memo, only to find something written in large text on the bottom.

"Stockings? Um… Fifty of them? What will you do with fifty stockings?"

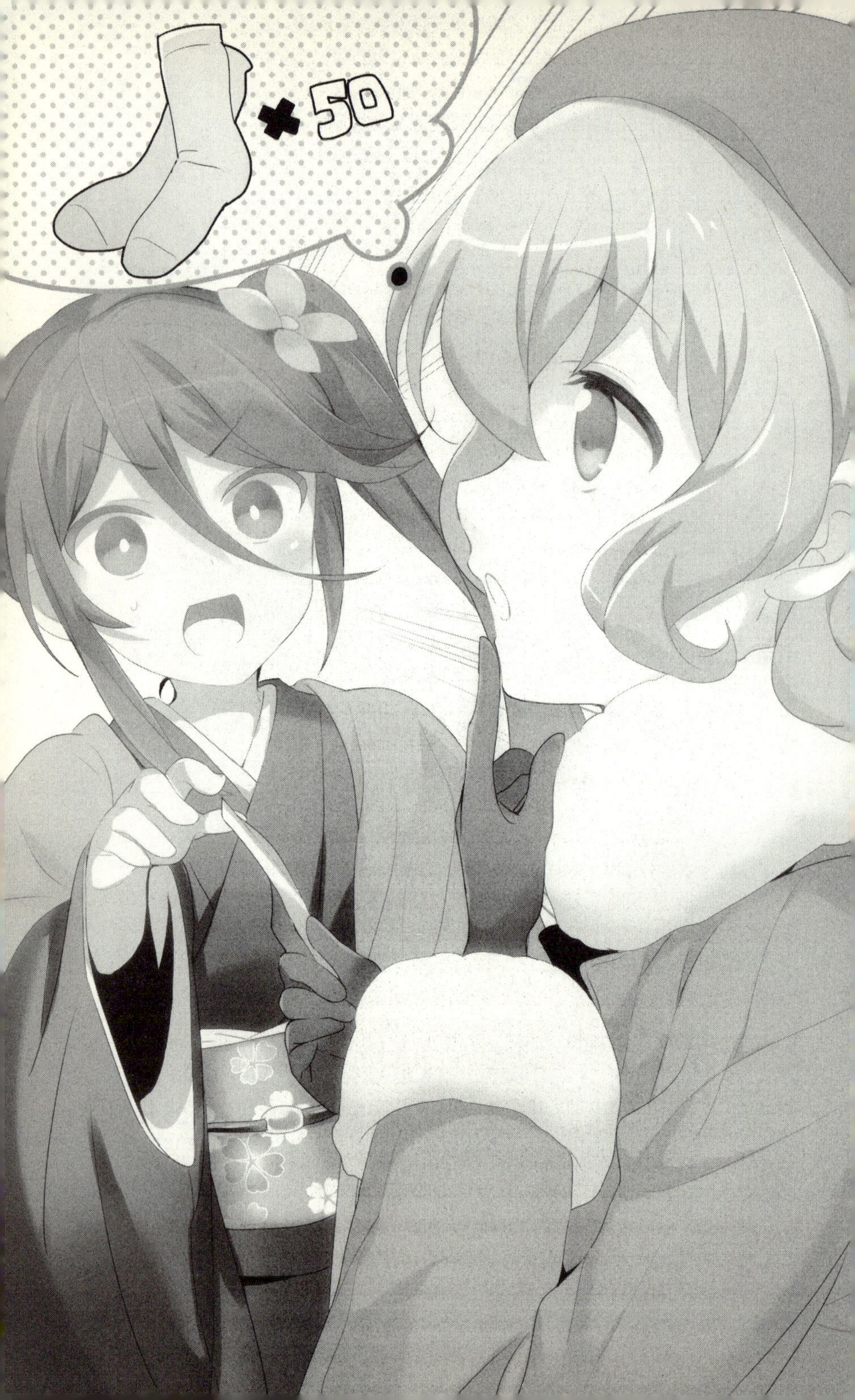
× 50

"Huhhh? But stockings are must-have items for thiiis time of year."

"As souvenirs?"

"Oh, yesss! Chriiistmas is a time when you give presents to someone you looove, and presents go inside stockings. That's a ruuule!"

"E-Emeralda, wait a minute! I think you are mixing up your facts!"

"Hmmm?"

Suzuno breathed a silent sigh of relief that she had noticed the mistake before any money had managed to exchange hands.

"As the tradition holds, Emeralda, it is Santa Claus who puts gifts in stockings for good little children. Just him! And that *only* applies to children, I should add!"

"Huhhhhhh?!"

The gasp was loud enough to make passersby stop and gawk.

"Besides, we are on our way to the UniClo by the Shinjuku Station west exit, are we not? I am not sure they sell the kind of stockings you can insert presents in. Er…probably."

She had not seen many of them herself, but Suzuno assumed that a discount clothing store would not be the right place to find the festive stockings Emeralda was likely imagining.

"Oh, dear, have I been making a mistaaake?"

"You have. Or not a mistake so much as mixing things up a bit. But yes, adults exchange presents with one another as well. Why not buy a few Japanese souvenirs for the trip back? You can have them gift wrapped for Christmas easily enough."

"Hmm…mmmm, I'm not suuure…"

"About what?"

"Here I thought that my presents needed to be these small oblong thiiings so they'd fit in the stockings. So I asked Emilia to buy some local wine for meee on the Net."

"…Oh."

As Emeralda quivered with concern, Suzuno racked her brain to recall what shopping on the Internet was like.

"And they did not gift wrap it for you?"

"I didn't aaask. I thought you put it in the stooocking."

"And the Western Island's current season... No, that will not work. The Nativity Festival is close at hand there as well. It is no time for a court sorcerer like yourself to go around with bottles of wine."

"Nooo, so I thought I would hide it in the stockings thiiis culture has..."

"Enough about stockings. Nobody in the court knows about this world apart from Albert and General Rumack in the first place. How did you plan to explain the custom of putting wine bottles in stockings?"

"Ah..."

Emeralda's face had an *I didn't think about that* expression written all over it.

"For now, perhaps we could buy some festive packaging? There may even be some wine gift packs you could purchase."

"A-all riiight..."

As she looked at the utterly abashed Emeralda, Suzuno couldn't shake the feeling that she saw someone make a similar mistake before. She searched her memory to figure out who it was as she walked around, looking for gift wrapping. Then, as they passed by a MgRonald, she realized something: Emeralda now was essentially Suzuno herself six months ago, performing the Obon festival in all the wrong ways and getting reamed by Maou for it.

"Belll?"

"Oh, no, er, I was just marveling at how far along I have come."

She wasn't karate-chopping Emeralda the way Maou did to her, but she was confident that she had grown used to life in Japan far faster than Maou or Emi did. She received a great deal of support from them, of course, not to mention Ashiya and Urushihara and Emi and Chiho. But it had still been less than a year since Sariel and the Church duped her into fighting against Maou and Emi.

"How many people do you plan to give gifts to, Emeralda?"

"Umm, not thaaat many..."

She counted on her fingers as they got on the elevator. It wasn't too many after all; Emeralda was really mostly buying things for herself.

Realizing that, Suzuno finally felt comfortable giving her some more casual advice.

"Thank you so muuuch for your help! I thiiiink I can save face with theeese gifts…"

They had gone on a little shopping spree in the end, bouncing from wrapping paper to this and that thing. It was morning when they began, but by now dusk was about to arrive. Their hands were full of shopping bags, and not even that was everything they had bought—a decent amount was on its way to Emi's place.

"Th-this is fine and all," Suzuno said as a beaming Emeralda bowed at her, "but…are you sure this is all right? Providing these sorts of souvenirs to General Rumack?"

Her main concern was the giant Relax-a-Bear doll they had won at a skill crane game at the arcade.

"Oh, of courrrse! She may not look it, but she loooves cute stuff."

"Wh-what a surprise…"

For Hazel Rumack, young commander in chief of the Saint Aile knights and key leader of the Federated Order of the Five Continents currently rebuilding the Central Continent, to like cute things was a shock. The fact that Emeralda had scored this enormous plushie after just three hundred yen's worth of playing was another.

"You have a thing for cute stuff, too, don't youuu, Bell?"

"Well, yes, but not quite like this, perhaps…"

"And providing gifts like theeese to the right peeeople will help procure the buuudget we need for the neeext year."

Suzuno scowled at the idea of a bright, overstuffed bear serving as an advanced tool of political negotiation. Wouldn't this technically count as bribery? Although she had once handled most of the Church's dirty work, she would have preferred—she thought as she looked into Relax-a-Bear's drooping eyes—that the "clean" members of the clergy kept themselves that way.

"Hmm? What's this?"

Then Suzuno looked up, noticing a familiar building.

"Ah, yes. Emeralda, this is the office that Emilia used to work in."

"Oh, reeeally?"

She tilted her head upward, Relax-a-Bear still in hand, as she spotted the Dokodemo sign at the very top.

"So is Rika here, too?"

"I suppose she could be. Whether she is on duty today, I cannot say."

Suzuno did hear that Rika helped Ashiya procure a smartphone recently. This they did alone together, unlike the television purchase of a while back. She thought a bit about Rika's behavior during that TV run but quickly shook her head.

"...No. Impossible. Not Alciel and Rika, of all people."

No, Rika looked like too upright of a woman for that, and unlike back then, she was now fully aware of Ashiya's true nature. That included the evil Ashiya had gotten up to on Ente Isla, of course, and Rika couldn't have been the type of woman to remain true to him after that...

"Ngh."

Then she recalled someone near and dear to them all, who remained true to the Devil King despite knowing everything about him and his past. She attempted to douse her imagination before the fire spread any further.

"Belll?"

"No, but Alciel did return home before too late on that day, and I do not believe Rika has been back to the apartment since..."

"Um, Bell, are youuu...?"

"H-however, the Devil King has appeared awfully busy as of late and the other demons have exhibited some strange behavior... Could it be...?"

"Ohhh, Bell!"

"Hmmm? What is it?"

"There! Over therrre."

"Mm?"

"It's Rikaaa."

"What?!"

Suzuno looked up to find Rika Suzuki waving her hand from across the street. She usually got out of work about now, so walking past her office at this time of day made this encounter less unlikely than one would expect.

Rika gestured at them to wait there and walked to a nearby crosswalk. Only when she began to cross did Suzuno realize that someone else was behind her—someone unfamiliar. A coworker, perhaps?

"Wow, Suzuno! What's with all that stuff you and Emeralda are carrying? You must've shopped 'til you dropped today!"

The Rika who arrived seemed just like the one both of them were familiar with. "Oh, where's Emi? Not with you today?"

"No… Unforrrtunately, I need to return home as soon as possible."

"Oh, really? Um… Back to your, uh, family's place?"

Rika spent a moment considering the figure following her before choosing that turn of phrase. It signaled to the Ente Islans that the woman behind her wasn't aware of who they were.

"Indeed, and I thought I would purchase some souveniiirs for the trip back, but Emiii said she couldn't escape work duties todaaay, so…"

Understanding Rika's intention, Emeralda made a point to use the name Emilia went by in Japan.

"Thus, I have Suuuzuno here showing me around instead."

"Oh, I see. Kinda sudden, though, isn't it?"

"No, not exaaactly. I really should have been home sooner than this aaactually."

"Yeah? But you'll be back, right?"

"Ohh, that depennnds…"

Life as a court official usually meant *Okay, the job's done. I'm gonna take off for a month* didn't fly with the upper management. Plus, depending on Emi and Laila's future relationship, Emeralda might be forced to shoulder the most difficult responsibility of any politician in Ente Isla. Japan tourism was pretty low on the priority list for the time being.

"Y'know, I was actually back at my parents' old place until the day before yesterday, too. I only got back to work yesterday. Good thing I got to say hello to you before you left!"

"Your parents' old place?"

"Yeah, over in Kobe! I hadn't been back in 'round two years. Time sure flies when you're having fun and stuff… Oh, right!"

Rika finally recalled the woman twiddling her thumbs behind her. "This is Maki Shimizu. She came on the job after me and Emi did. Maki, this is Emi's friend Suzuno Kamazuki and, um…"

She paused for a moment, unsure whether to introduce Emeralda as is. Emeralda picked up the sign.

"My name is Emeralda Etuuuva. I knew Emi back when we were in class togetherrr."

"Oh, right," the woman said, "Emi mentioned you were staying at her place for a little while. My name's Maki Shimizu! It was great hanging out with Yusa and Sasaki earlier!"

""Sasaki?""

Suzuno and Emeralda looked at each other, not expecting the name.

"She means Chiho," Rika explained. "Maki knows her, actually."

"Actually, it was you, Rika, who told Sasaki about me! That's why she came over!"

Maki seemed unnaturally excited about this, balling up her fists and everything. If she knew Emi and Rika, then maybe it wasn't so odd that Chiho was part of their circle. But why was she acting so deferential to Sasaki despite clearly being older?

"Oh, wait, were youuu the person Emi mentioned to meee?"

"You guys know Sasaki as well?"

"I do."

"Yesss!"

"So how have Yusa and Sasaki been since?"

"How?" Suzuno wondered, unsure what Maki meant.

"I guess," Rika explained, "Emi and Chiho went to Maki's place and talked about career advancement for a while."

""Career advancement?""

"Uh-huh!" Maki agreed. "Yusa was staying over for a couple of nights, but I guess she had a few questions about going to college at that time, so I gave her all the advice I could about that. Sasaki joined us on the second day, and I guess she was worried about what to do after high school as well, so I worked with her through a few things, too!"

"Emi did that...?"

"Wow, college, huuuh? College in Japaaan?"

"Yes! We were looking at a few different agricultural schools."

Suzuno and Emeralda were, by coincidence, both picturing the same thing: *So she wasn't accepting Laila's request...?*

They couldn't say how serious Emi was about university studies, but she had always talked about taking useful, advanced things from Earth and bringing them to Ente Isla. Her chance encounter with Nord on Earth also gave her a more concrete goal in life—to rebuild her home village. It was only natural for the daughter of a wheat-growing family to pursue higher education in agriculture, and if that was what she wanted, she was bound to learn far more in Japan than at a school back home. Japan's universities generally ran for four years, too, so if this was the path she wanted to take, it meant she'd have to stay in this country for at least five more years.

Emeralda appraised the news with a natural smile. "If thaaat's what she waaants, then I would aaabsolutely support it, yes."

"Emeralda...?"

"Perrrsonally, I would put Emi's life ahead of pretty much aaanyone in the world...including her own faaamily."

She was expressing her own resolve there, in ways Rika and Maki wouldn't have seen. At that MozzBurger in Nerima, she had learned the full nature and the cause of the threat facing Ente Isla from Gabriel. Even with that in mind, though, Emeralda wanted to put her full, unflagging support behind Emi pursuing her own happiness.

"And if anyone gets in Emi's waaay, I'll gladly risk my liiife to take care of them. With all the hope you've showed her, Makiii, I think Emi needs to take advaaantage of that."

"Yes," Suzuno agreed, "I am now fully aware of the strength of your drive, Emeralda. And I am sure going to school with Chiho would be even more attractive to her."

"Mmm, well, unless they pursue the same major, they'll probably wind up in different schools, or departments, or whatever. Staying together can be a lot harder than it sounds." Maki grinned a little. "Oh, but it seemed to me Sasaki was considering a third option besides school or work, and she seemed kind of motivated in *that* direction, too, if you know what I mean…"

Suzuno and Emeralda didn't.

"Oh, quit being mean," Rika replied with a grin.

"Aw, but you knowww…" Maki's eyes seemed to sparkle as she smiled. "Isn't it fascinating to see? I mean, if you know these two girls, then of *course* you're gonna be interested in the guy both of them have in their sights."

""…!!""

Suzuno and Emeralda tried their hardest not to gasp right there. She had to be talking about Maou, even if the women had him "in their sights" for very different reasons. What kind of advice had Emi and Chiho been asking Maki for anyway?

"And that little girl Alas Ramus called him something different, but the way she saw him as his daddy tells me that he and Emi have a pretty close thing going!"

Suzuno and Emeralda broke into a cold sweat. Maki was both wrong and dangerously *not* wrong at the same time. It wasn't their position to butt in on his personal life, but there was no way letting yet more Earth natives in on the secret behind Maou and Emi would accomplish anything for anyone on either side. They'd prefer if Emi actively worked to avoid that, but she had a tendency to leave her sides open sometimes—a bit like her mother, actually.

As they thought about this, Rika raised a hand. "Oh, that reminds me—if Emi's working but you two are out on the town, then who's watching Alas Ramus?"

"Oh, right. She is with Ashiya, so I could guide Emeralda around."

"Ahh, I see. Well, she'll be fine with him, huh? Is he getting along okay with his new phone?"

"The one you helped him find?"

"Yeah, kinda."

"Well, I do not interact with him very much, but he did say the phone makes it easier to reach people."

"Oh? That's good." Rika smiled a little and turned to Maki. "Okay, Maki, unless you wanna keep poking this horse until you get kicked, let's leave it at that for now. I'm gonna hang out with you all day today, remember?"

Maki greeted this with great reluctance. "Huh? I—I didn't mean to poke anyone…"

Rika's breezy smile turned into a mask of terror. "Right! In that case, we're gonna go all night! Tonight, Maki, I'm gonna be a horde of zombies, and you're gonna be the hapless citizens caught in my swarm! You better be ready!"

"Huh? Oh, uh… Umm? Wait! Hey, how about you two join us, huh?!"

""What?""

Maki, realizing what she had just gotten herself into, turned to Suzuno and Emeralda for help. Rika stopped her.

"No running away! Those two have their own business to attend to. I'm gonna teach you that loose lips sink ships tonight—the *hard* way, got it? So get on home for now, but don't think that means I'm letting you go!"

"Yeahhh…"

"Okay, guys, sorry to hold you up. Lemme know if you find out what day you're leaving, Emeralda. I'd like to see you off if I'm free."

"C-certainly."

"Yesss! I will!"

Grabbing the mysterious thunderstorm that was Maki, Rika waved at the two and began to set off. She only made it a few steps before stopping. "Tell Emi," she said without turning around, "that I think I can talk calmly about things when a little bit more time has passed, okay? For now, see you!"

"Um, yeah, sorry! See you later sometime!"

Without waiting for a response, she took the shouting Maki into the Shinjuku crowds, leaving the two of them thoroughly confused among the evening retail traffic.

"What was thaaat all about?"

"I cannot say. I cannot say, but…"

But it couldn't have been her imagination. The moment Ashiya's name came up, there was something almost painfully sad to Rika's smile.

Suzuno had been aware of Rika's feelings toward Ashiya well before now. The anxiety she had felt a moment ago wasn't just her imagination; something truly dramatic must have happened between those two…

"There is little point dwelling on the topic. But…but…"

But Suzuno could also see how Chiho and Maou's relationship could easily turn out like Rika and Ashiya's. And right now, Laila and her pleas were a wedge dividing the humans and the demons. As of this minute, Suzuno doubted either Maou or Emi would accept Laila and Gabriel's offer. Despite everything about the past they had revealed, they still shared similar opinions as Chiho and Urushihara—no matter how tragedy laden the past was and no matter how strongly it was impacting this world, none of it was related to Maou's and Emi's current lives. It was a simple matter of whether their interactions with Laila inspired them to adjust their schedules at all—and right now, both of those schedules were heavily aligned toward Japan.

This did not mean Suzuno didn't have her misgivings. Chiho—unable to fight, unable to decide her own path for herself—was troubled by Laila's presence. It made her doubt her position with Maou, and she was seeking answers. If she decided to confront Maou and demand a yes-or-no decision, Suzuno couldn't begin to guess which way Maou's internal scales would tip. If it was Sadao Maou, he'd likely be of the same heart and willing to accept Chiho. If it was

Satan the Devil King, he'd likely feel more responsibility for all the demons scattered by the failed attack on Ente Isla.

Suzuno was with Maou the whole way during their Ente Islan rescue effort, and that was exactly why she found him impossible to read. In particular, her main concern was that accepting Chiho's feelings may not necessarily mean wanting to live with Chiho.

"He can be surprisingly elusive…"

"Hmm? Who isss?"

"Mm, um, no, nothing…"

"Rika sure acted like something was up with herrr."

"Who can say? It did not seem like something to prod her about."

"Hmmmm…"

"What?"

Emeralda thought for a moment, staring at the crowds of people Rika and Maki had melted into.

"Maaaybe I shouldn't go home aaafter all."

"What?!" Suzuno blurted. This was sudden news. "Can—can you really do that? Simply say *oh, never mind* to it?"

"Oh, I thiiink I can. I have a feeling going home would be a baaad idea right nowww, you know."

"A bad idea? I thought you had to go home!"

"Aw, but it'd be such a waaasted opportunity if I left!"

"Wasted…? You do understand Christmas will come again next year, yes?"

"Assuming there is a next yeeear."

"Huh?!" The assertion Emeralda casually tossed out stopped Suzuno in her tracks.

"Do you think there will be?"

"No, I…I mean…"

"If the Devil King and Emilia accept that offer, then Ms. Sasaki is right. There is no telling how much time it would take. Depending on what all three of them opt to do, we may never have a chance to celebrate Christmas in Japan again."

Suzuno had nothing to counter Emeralda's words, delivered sternly but with the same cute little face as always.

"That's why I can't afford to leave Japan yet. Emilia wants to remain here—listening to Rika and Maki affirmed that much to me. Emilia isn't the type of girl to struggle against something she knows there is no hope of achieving. But there she apparently was, at Maki's house, trying to examine her dreams without my knowledge. She wants to stay here, and if she does, I have to stand by her side and support her along the way…so I can enjoy Christmas here next year and the year after that."

She looked up at Suzuno, the smile returning to her face.

"Sooo let's have as muuuch fun as we can with Emiiilia this Christmaaas! Come on! Change of plaaans! Let's buy presents to hand out to evvveryone!"

"What?! W-wait a moment! But Albert in Saint Aile…"

"That's none of my busssiness. I'll just send all our souvenirs through a Gaaate to apologize. Now, we need a gift for Alas Raaamus first. That girl still isn't very uuused to me."

"Ah?! You intend to shop *more*?!"

"Christmas presents are meant for chillldren first and foremost, right? I think you would know more about what she liiikes, Bell."

"N-no, wait, wait a moment! Are you quite sure about this?!"

"Hee-hee-hee! Oh, I can't wait to toast with champagne and wine, as we enjoy our roast turrrkey, and Scotch eggs, and tuna suuushi, and fried shrimp, and sweet potaaatoes, and fancy caaake!"

"You are mixing in a few odd choices there, Emeralda! Wait a minute!"

Suzuno was forced to give chase to Emeralda, already lost in her own little retail world. Round two of her shopping spree went on for two more hours, and by the time Suzuno made it back home, she barely had the energy to speak.

"Wow, Bell, my dude, are you really a person with that little stamina?"

"No, no, the issue has nothing to do with stamina…"

"My liege tells me that you engaged in similar feats of shopping when you first arrived here. Is that right?"

"No, it is nothing to do with that."

"Sleep well, Suzu-Sis!"

Suzuno, fresh from being dragged around Shinjuku all day, was slumped against the table at Room 201. The thought of the day's events, brought back to her memory even more vividly by Urushihara, Ashiya, and Alas Ramus's questions respectively, only added to her weariness.

"All the crowds drained me, you see. So much feverish enthusiasm…"

Whether it was a weekday or not, attempting to hit the shops around Shinjuku after five PM, carrying massive bags and boxes around with you, took a certain amount of resolve.

"So? Emeralda Etuva is back in Eifukucho, then? Emilia and His Demonic Highness are still at work, but why are you here?"

"Ahh…"

"Hm?"

In response to Ashiya's prodding, Suzuno turned an eye toward Alas Ramus, currently poised on top of Urushihara's shoulders as he tapped away at the computer.

"Call it a favor for Emeralda or an errand…" she said.

"Pardon?"

"Alas Ramus has never seemed very keen on her, you know…"

"What are you trying to say?" Ashiya asked as he peeled a potato.

"…My apologies. May I have a moment?"

Suzuno realized she needed to be more specific, but this wasn't something she wanted Alas Ramus eavesdropping on, so she reluctantly left the warm *kotatsu* table and called Ashiya to the walkway outside the apartment.

"So what?"

"Well… This is something I would normally need the Devil King and Emilia's permission to discuss…"

She revealed the whole story to Ashiya—that Emeralda wanted to buy a Christmas present for Alas Ramus so she'd like her more.

"She was ready to purchase one today, but we had little idea what Alas Ramus might enjoy, and well, we wanted to make sure everyone around her was on board."

"Hmm."

"The Devil King and Emilia both work on the twenty-fourth and twenty-fifth, correct?"

Ashiya nodded. "Ahh, I see what you mean now."

To everyone who hung around the apartment besides Chiho, Christmas was just another event on the holiday calendar in this alien world of Japan. The end of the year was simply a time when their work shifts got all messed up. The idea of Emeralda giving Alas Ramus a present seemed nothing but strange.

Still, teaching a child about traditional yearly events was an important thing. Showing them that certain days and seasons and city atmospheres were special helped establish them as customs in their minds, keeping the days special for their entire lives. But as mentioned, Christmas was a Japanese—okay, Earth—tradition, and nothing Suzuno or Ashiya deemed as particularly can't-miss. Suzuno's faith was for a different religion entirely, and a demon like Ashiya saw no reason to celebrate the birth of a holy figure in the first place.

"To be honest," admitted Suzuno, "I am unsure whether Christmas is a custom we should be teaching Alas Ramus."

"I understand that, but I see no reason to stop her. Do you?"

"Oh?"

"Emeralda Etuva giving Alas Ramus a present is nothing harmful, at least. If you think it is too early to delve into Christmas, we can just call it a present and leave it at that."

"You have a point, perhaps."

"On the other hand, if my liege or Emilia wish to teach Alas Ramus about Christmas, there is no reason to stop them, either. My liege and I went through the traditional custom of visiting a temple on New Year's Day last year, after all, albeit for rather different motives from most. As long as she lives here, she does have the right and the need to learn at least a few social norms."

Ashiya was making perfect sense, but Suzuno had a reason to be wary. It all boiled down to that one statement from Emeralda.

"But how long will she be living here?"

"Hmm?"

"Will there be a…next year, for example?"

"…What are you hinting at?" Ashiya flatly stated, averting his eyes from Suzuno's below. "You know our plans, and you know where my liege's career at MgRonald is going right now. He finally has a foothold on the position he has long dreamed of for himself in Japan. Do you think he will fritter away that opportunity and go off somewhere?"

"…Can I trust you on that?"

Ashiya gave Suzuno's brooding eyes a dubious look. "What? I assume you would prefer the two of them accept this request."

"Do not misjudge me," she spat out. "I am not in the habit of sacrificing the life of my friend."

"Then stop overthinking matters like this. If you and Emeralda wish to give Alas Ramus a present, then bring up the issue with Emilia, her…mother, of sorts."

"…All right. I will."

"Good. Is that all? I have a dinner to prepare." Ashiya turned around.

"Alciel?"

"Mm?" He winced as he was forced to turn back.

"I ran into Rika today in Shinjuku. She was worried about how well you were using your new telephone."

"…She was?"

Did she notice his expression changing just then? Whether she did or not, Suzuno could tell something substantial was taking place between the demon and the Earthling.

"You could try to contact her, you know."

"Indeed."

And with that, Ashiya went back inside, closing the door behind him and leaving Suzuno in the hallway.

"…What am I even doing?" she whispered to herself as she stood there, crestfallen. This whole business of fretting over whether to teach a baby about Christmas with a bunch of demons wasn't a joke. But the fact she could look back on this and other incidents and laugh about how "normal" it was or not tormented Suzuno. Somehow, she knew that the weird sense of comfort this apartment offered—a comfort that seemed ready to last forever—was about to fall apart. It didn't seem like Maou, Emi, and Laila had engaged in any secret negotiations since Nerima; they acted like there was nothing special about that day at all, in fact, apart from being toured around Laila's place.

"What…? What do I even want them to do?"

All the confusing feelings she couldn't put a name to were beginning to overwhelm her…

"Hmm? Suzuno? What are you doing in the outside here? Looking all the confused?"

Then she realized Acieth was right next to her, carrying with both hands a pair of corn dogs that she must've bought at some convenience store.

"Ah… Acieth. Is the Devil King finished with work?"

Suzuno looked around for Maou, the fatigue still written on her face, but he was nowhere to be found. He and Alas Ramus were connected, and like with Alas Ramus and Emi, they couldn't venture physically far from each other. It was safe for Acieth to hang around Sasazuka while Maou worked at the MgRonald in Hatagaya, but Maou's current full-time employee training would be taking place at assorted locations around Tokyo, none of them near here. Acieth would have to remain nearish, but Maou couldn't take her along for training with Kisaki around, so she remained fused within his body during the actual training sessions.

"No, not yet. But he is returned at MgRonald in Hatagaya. He took me out in dark spot, nobody can see, and I go home first. Ashiya, I imagine he is making the dinner now, yes?"

Unlike her big sister Alas Ramus, Acieth had almost no sense of self-control. The way Maou put it, she was unwilling to remain fused with his body for a single second longer than necessary.

Once he returned to Hatagaya, he probably couldn't wait to get rid of her.

"Yes, well, if you are here to enjoy dinner, why did you buy more food?"

"Mikitty told me. She said, if you eat outside of my pop or Mikitty's house, you go out and fill stomach a little first, before meal. Otherwise, much crying."

"Ah…"

It made sense to Suzuno. She had seen Ashiya almost erupt into tears several times after Acieth bugged him into making something, only to have her all but empty the refrigerator. Acieth, picking up on Suzuno's wonder, gave her a bit of a peeved look.

"Look, do I eat too much? Really?"

"Uh…"

Despite standing stationary, Suzuno was seized by the sense that she had just tripped over something. It must have shown on her face, because Acieth's changed to a look of resignation.

"Ohhh. So I do, yes?"

"A-Acieth?"

"I had the premonition that, yes, it is so."

Suzuno wasn't sure if Acieth really understood what *premonition* meant. In many ways, she didn't know what to say to her. As far as she had seen, Acieth didn't know what *enough* meant at the dining room table, either. It hadn't affected her figure at all, but not even the greatest lawyer in the universe could beat the charge that Acieth was an excessively gluttonous woman.

"Hmm… Perhaps we must talk with Maou about it?"

"Talk? Talk about what?"

"Things. Maybe, ah, Ashiya can buy more rice, or when fused together, he can eat twice as much, or he can buy me phone…"

There was a lot Suzuno could say about this—she still hadn't given up on the phone? Was this really a problem about portions? But she could tell that Maou wasn't going to give an inch on any of it.

"Mmm, yes, I think it will work. If I use my sister as shield, it is easy win against Maou!"

"That may be a double-edged sword, Acieth. Use it too much, and you will make enemies out of Emilia and Alciel, too."

She was aware that Acieth tended to use Alas Ramus as a handy tool for pushing her will on people. But in terms of Alas Ramus's future, nobody among their group could afford to cave in like that.

"We can hear you!" came Ashiya's voice from beyond the Room 201 door, making both Suzuno and Acieth draw back.

"Ooh, big failure, big failure. The walls here, they are very thin, yes? I must adjust my plans, so they will not know."

"Acieth…"

The sheer lack of remorse made even Suzuno wince.

"Yes, I know I eat without work even more than Lucifer, but now is best time to ask for things, no? I will not give up!"

"The best time? Hmm?"

"Yes! Maou, he may play the dumb, but I know! In Christmas, we all eat big meal!"

"Oh… Oh."

As she dodged a drop of ketchup that dripped off one of Acieth's corn dogs, Suzuno thought she could detect every man inside Room 201 gasping in distress. She pretended to hear nothing.

"W-wait a minute, Acieth! At least finish what you brought here first! A ketchup stain on this kimono would be an incredible pain to wash out! And do not discuss such things in front of Alas Ramus!"

"What, corn dogs?"

"Christmas!"

Suzuno quickly lowered her voice, realizing it was growing louder than Acieth's, and brought her lips to her ear.

"Um… Alas Ramus knows nothing about Christmas. If we wish to do something for her, best to keep it a secret until just before, for the sake of the surprise."

"Oh! I see! Yes, a surprise!"

She had just been talking about Christmas with Ashiya, but Suzuno knew the best way to convince Acieth to do something was to make it seem fun for her. If she thought Alas Ramus would like it more, this should make it easy to keep her from yapping about the holiday until the day actually came.

"All right! Then I will do the talking with Maou about that, too. He seems stressed since he handles all the new things right now, so I need to wait until he is the serene again..."

Acieth looked deadly serious. The upper half of her face did anyway, with the bottom busily devouring two corn dogs at once in an astonishing feat of flexibility. In a short time, all she had left were the sticks.

"Anyway! We will surprise big sis! I hear you the loud and clear! So, Suzuno, what are you thinking?"

"Huh?! Um, we—we were still planning matters, but Emeralda is quite enthused about it all..."

She was too flustered by the sudden question not to mention Emeralda. It wasn't a lie, but if Acieth came to know that other people were also planning for Christmas, it could prove even trickier to make her butt out. But there was no taking it back. Acieth's eyes began to burn with raging flame, raising a corn dog stick high in the air like a Hero's sword.

"Hngh! I am the more excited than ever! And now I am the hungry!"

"Wha—?!"

"Bell! Damn you! I will make you pay for this!"

"Ashiya! Maou will be the home soon! What's for dinner?!"

Once Ashiya began griping at them from the kitchen window, Acieth hurriedly stormed inside Room 201.

"Such a fearsome storm this is..."

The storm subsiding from Suzuno's sight was now bearing down upon Room 201 itself.

"...So be it. I do owe Alciel for this. If the Devil King is returning soon, I could at least offer a few things for the dinner table."

Whether it was thanks to Acieth or the fault of Acieth, Suzuno was finally able to switch mental gears. She hurried back to Room 202 before she had to endure the screams of Ashiya that would no doubt be coming along shortly.

✳

Several hours had passed since Acieth's sudden attack on the Devil's Castle dinner plans. It was late at night, Alas Ramus sleeping peacefully on the bed in Emi's apartment in Eifukucho.

Meanwhile, Emi was curled up on the floor nearby with her head in her hands, Emeralda kneeling down and trying to offer comfort.

"Now, now, there is no need to feel so down about thiiis…"

"How could I *not* be down about it?"

"There's no way around it. You're going through a great deeeeal, Emi, and this isn't a custom that one sees in Ente Isla…"

"That isn't the problem." Emi groaned, keeping her head down. "No matter how hard it is or isn't for me, that doesn't mean I'm safe to avoid thinking about Alas Ramus… She's had it as hard as I have."

She put her head up, flattening out the shift schedule she had all but pulverized in her fist a moment ago.

"Ohhh, what have I done?"

How shallow she must have been a month ago! Both she and Maou were on duty for December 24 and December 25.

"Ugghh…"

She balled herself up again.

"Maaaybe I shouldn't have saaaid anything?" Emeralda said, a little unnerved at this dramatic reaction.

Emi had returned to her apartment after picking up Alas Ramus from Devil's Castle, and Emeralda had waited for Emi to put her to sleep before asking if she could give her a gift. It was a simple question—nothing meant behind it—but it made Emi freeze in place.

"Christ…mas?"

"Er, yes! Ummm, I heard it celebrates the birrrth of a holy figure here on Earrrth?"

"Christ…mas?"

"E-Emilia?"

"When is Christmas?!"

Then she let out a scream that, barring a miracle, absolutely had to have woken up Alas Ramus. She had run off to her calendar, checked her shift schedule—and it had been like this ever since.

"It… It didn't matter at all to me last year, so…!"

"E-Emiliaaa? You can't torrrture yourself like this…"

"How did I not notice until today…? I could have picked up on it in a million different ways before now! When I made my shift requests, when she printed out the schedules, when Sariel started freaking out about Sentucky starting their Christmas reservations…"

"Yesss, perhaps you should have noooticed at one point or the other…"

Even Emeralda had to chuckle a little at Sariel's name coming up.

"I mean, this is supposed to be a religious holiday, right? I didn't realize it'd be this huge party for everybody. I thought it was kind of weird last year, like…I bought a little cake and stuff, at the nearby convenience store since they had a deal going, but it didn't feel like anything special…so…"

"Well, you've been buuusy! Lately, you've just been cycling between your house, that aparrrtment building, and work, haven't you? Maybe you didn't see too many of the decoraaations in town."

"And everybody on crew has to wear Santa hats starting tomorrow… Ugh, geez!"

Emi had not wholly forgotten about Christmas. It was just that last year's experience had given her such a skewed idea of the holiday that she didn't realize it was for celebrating and having fun with people. The main thing she remembered about it was how surprised she was that all the public décor switched from Christmas to New Year's by the morning of December 26.

"It's all riiight! We could always hold the festivities on another daaay, can't we? It's not like we are involved with the religious aaaspect of it…"

"We aren't. No, you're right. But… I wanted to tell Alas Ramus about all this fun stuff coming up for her, and right at the start, I'm screwing it up… Uggh…"

"Ummm…"

Emeralda looked a little surprised by this. "So you wanted to teach her about Chriiistmas?"

"Yeah."

"Which meeeans that you intend to celebrate it again next yeeear?"

"...Yeah."

"............Which meeeeeeeeeans—"

"There's no deeper meaning to it." With a sigh, Emi finally sat back up. "I have no idea where Alas Ramus and I are going to be by the time it's December twenty-fifth again on Earth. Remember, this time last year, I was intent on slaying the Devil King and going back to Ente Isla. The year before that was bloody warfare. By this time next year, I know I'll look back on agonizing about my Christmas shift schedule and just laugh about it."

"...But you'll be together with her this time next yeeear, won't you?"

"...Yeah."

"And anybody eeelse?"

"Everyone."

"Eeeveryone?"

"Everyone. Everyone I hold dear to me at that time."

Emi stood up, fished her smartphone out of her bag, and placed a call.

"Hello? Hey. You got a moment? I hear crying in the background... Oh, Acieth is there for dinner? Well, you have my condolences."

If Acieth's name came up, Emeralda assumed she was talking to somebody living in Villa Rosa Sasazuka.

"So I wanted to talk to you about Christmas... No, we got just barely enough people, so I can't request a shift change now. Eme told me... Oh, you heard, too? Okay... Yeah, I feel the same way. But anyway, it all got started because Eme wanted to give a Christmas present to Alas Ramus... Right. Yeah. So we can't do the day of, but if we could do it on the twenty-third or twenty-sixth, then at least one of us could be on hand for it, so I thought, like, maybe we could do something?"

This astonished Emeralda a little. Emi was talking to Maou. The "us" in "at least one of us" had to include him. She watched as Emi listened silently for a bit.

"Yeah. Yeah… Huh?! Uh, wait a minute, I didn't say anything to Chiho. Huh? Why? …I mean, anything's fine! We can work out things with her later but not right this minute! I can bring it up with her first, so please don't say anything when you see her tomorrow, all right?"

Maou must've suggested that they discuss matters with Chiho, a proposal that immediately set off alarm bells with Emi for reasons Emeralda couldn't guess from her perspective.

"Eme? Yeah, it's sounding like she's not leaving after all. I dunno why, but she says everything is all right, so… Okay. Right, I'll talk to you later."

The several-minutes-long conversation came to a close, with neither side raising their voices.

"Was that the Devil King?"

"Yeah. He was kinda pissed since he was about to go to sleep."

Emeralda wondered why there'd be crying in the background while Maou was trying to sleep, but Emi didn't explain why. Instead she turned toward Alas Ramus, sleeping in her bed with her arms outstretched.

"I think he understood what I was getting at. But he's a demon, you know? The thought of celebrating Christmas with Alas Ramus never even occurred to him, so he got kind of whiny about that."

"Whiiiny?"

"Well, you know, whenever Alas Ramus is involved…" Emi connected her phone to its charger, placed it on the table, and heaved a dejected sigh. "The Devil King's busy right now, so even though he saw Christmas on the calendar, I guess he didn't realize how close it really was. He only really thought of it as a day when people ate lots of cake and cookies—that was his attempt at an excuse."

"I thought MgRonald only made cakes for birrrthdays."

"He wasn't on shift that day last year, so apparently he and Alciel picked up a one-day job selling Christmas cakes at some convenience store." Emi looked back at her wadded-up shift schedule.

"Chiho is off on the twenty-fourth…but unlike our last birthday party, the Devil King doesn't really know where his training is yet. It might not necessarily be at his home location."

"But if you and the Devil King are together with Alas Ramus and she calls you Mommy, that will cause quite the paaanic in the ressstaurant, no?"

"Yeah. And some of the more senior crewmembers are on that day's shift, so we can't really pull the gray-area stuff we did with the birthday party. What should we do…?"

Emi's eyes turned toward a photo frame propped on top of her clothes dresser, one of the gifts she received during her and Chiho's tandem birthday party in October. It held a photo of everyone at the party, except Maou, centered around the two birthday girls. Maou steadfastly refused to join the shot, so he took the picture instead. Ashiya offered to do it for him, but Maou had shot him down—he was on the clock and in uniform, so if the wrong person saw the photo, he could get in trouble.

Emeralda followed Emi's eyes toward the photo and to the smiling Chiho posed next to her in it.

"So why can't you discuss matters with Ms. Sasaaaki? I think it'd be better to ask herrr for advice, rather than flounder around with what little Christmas knowledge we haaave…"

"Ahh………well…"

Emi opened her mouth but had trouble piecing the words together. She was even starting to blush.

"Um… Well, maybe I'm overthinking it, or being too self-conscious, or something like that…"

"Oh?"

"It's like, lately things haven't been going quite right between me and Chiho a little."

"Reeeally?! Did—did you and Ms. Sasaki have an arrrgument?!"

This was honestly a shock to Emeralda. She didn't know Chiho that well, but even then, it was impossible to imagine anything that would make them butt heads with each other.

"No, not like that. We still talk all the time; there haven't been any fights or anything. But, like, when the subject turns to Alas Ramus, she can't talk about anything unless the Devil King's involved. So asking Chiho from the very start about what we should do is, to me...you know..."

"Ohhh? I'm not sure I know at all, no."

"Mmm, how should I put it? Ugh, and now I'm breaking out into this weird sweat."

"Emiliaaa? You're acting weeeird."

"I know I'm acting weird. Like, more than you'd ever know! I just mean..."

She *was* sweating despite the cold, fanning herself with one hand and using the other to grab the AC remote and look at the temperature.

"...Back with all that stuff on the Eastern Island, you know, the Devil King helped out a ton, right?"

"Truuue."

"So now I'm one of the new crewmembers at MgRonald, and he's the one training me. He's shift supervisor, so that's pretty much a given."

"Uh-huhhh..."

"So then Laila shows up, and then I've been doing all this irresponsible stuff, right?"

"I cannot denyyy that, no."

"Right? So... Ugghhh..." Emi groaned—out of regret, or out of fatigue, or maybe to round up her disorganized feelings. "The Devil King's been...so damn nice to me the whole time."

"...............................Hmm?" Emeralda's eyes shot open.

"So... You know... Chiho's gotten kind of...kind of jealous."

"Hmmmm?"

"Before we went to Laila's place, me and the Devil King... Some, um, stuff happened..."

"Hmmmmmmmmmmmmmmmmmmmmmmmmmmmmmmmmmmm-mmmmmmmmmm??"

Whether she understood what this meant or not, Emeralda was now half off her seat, with Emi holding her head and trying her hardest to dodge her intent glare.

"Emilia?" She brought herself toward Emi's ear, her voice low. "What do you want to hear from me?"

"...Um."

Emi clammed up for a good half minute. Then in a barely audible whisper:

"...I don't know."

"Then can I give you my honest feelings?"

"...Okay."

"Depending on the circumstances, I may need to leave right now and go slay the Demon King."

Emeralda's voice indicated how serious she was.

"The way you're acting right now is like nothing I've seen from you before, Emilia. Depending on what's causing it, I believe I will need to contact several related parties."

"......Er."

"I am feeling very emotional right now. Beyond whatever we've discussed before, I need to know what happened. This...'stuff' between you and him."

"W-wait! Not—not that! Nothing weird or anything...!"

The veiled accusation made Emi flash back to that night, the infamous evening her head kept spitting out system errors. It made her blush a shade redder than before, and Emeralda wasn't blind to it.

"There was some stuff, you say, involved, which made Chiho jealous enough that even you picked up on it. That alone is enough to summon a mighty tempest in my heart. I find it hard to remain calm."

"I-I'm serious! Nothing happened! It was a huge pile of nothing!"

"Then please tell me. You can talk about it if it was nothing, can't you? What did that crude and disgusting demon do to my beloved Emilia?"

"I—I *told* you, nothing!"

"You're going to wake up Alas Ramus. Please be quiet."

"I—I can't because you're putting the screws on me, all right? I'll tell you! Please step back a little!"

Emeralda heeded the half-screamed order, kneeling on the ground just a short distance away and looking straight at Emi.

"Now, listen, I swear to you nothing happened..."

It was with an unsteady voice that Emi began to explain all the events of that night. Those eyes of hers were just too scary to deal with. But by the end of it:

"Haaaaaaa... This is sooo ridiiiculous..."

Emeralda was far looser now, the accusatory light in her eyes replaced with exasperation. By the end of it, she was lying on the ground and enjoying some crackers as she listened.

"Did you knowww, Emilia? On Earth, they call that Stockholm syndrooome."

Meanwhile, Emi felt like her rising temperature mixed with the cold sweat was going to turn her into a puddle of goo.

"And you knowww, no matter how casually friendly I've come to be with the Devil Kiiing, if something happened between you twooo, not that I really thought sooo, but if it diiid—and wow, as grown-up as Ms. Sasaki seems, she's still just a kiiid, too, huh?"

It was a funny thing to hear, given how much older Emeralda looked than even Chiho.

"But I could perhaps understaaand that, given the Devil King's personaaality, right? It's all thiiings that would be good for Alas Ramus more than youuu, so what's the big deeeal? Except for that paaart where you had to huuug him and stuuuff..."

"Nnnnnnngh."

Emi wanted more than anything to melt, evaporate, and vanish for good from the world right now.

"I don't see aaanything for Ms. Sasaki to be jealous about, thooough."

"B-but that's what Laila and the Devil King said."

"Well, you and the Devil King were pretty diiistant before now, so even if you act norrrmally with each other, it could looook like things have changed quite a biiit."

"Ugh... Well, maybe so..."

"So ridiiiculous... Ridiiiculous..."

"Can you stop calling it ridiculous over and over?! This is freaking me out, too!"

"Ahh, I see Ente Isla committed a great criiime in stealing away your youuuth. You were out journeying so long, and the only maaale accompaniment was a burly giant and this ooold guy..."

Now Emi could see it. Emeralda was exasperated with her in just the same way Laila was. But in her eyes, being told that over and over again wasn't going to achieve much for her at this point.

"But if thaaat's how it is, I can see how it'd be difficult to sit down and taaalk over matters with Ms. Sasaki. You can't just go up to her and say *I'm busy with worrrk, so can you hold a Christmas party with the daaaughter of the guy you got the hots for,* caaan you?"

"Eme!!"

Emeralda's frankness led Emilia to shout the word in a mixture of anger and surprise.

"Nmmghm..."

"Ah...!"

But Alas Ramus grimaced in her sleep and turned on her side, so Emi quickly shut her mouth.

"All riiight... In thaaat case—well, I suggested this firrrst, so I'll find a way to discuss this with Ms. Sasaki... Bell, too, of courrrse."

"Oh? You will?"

"Ahhh... Perhaps we should contact Riiika as well? She would have quite a nummmber of ideas for a birthday party, I'm suuure..."

"Um... Well, I mean, Rika..."

"Mmm? Are things awwwkward with Rika, too?"

"N-no, but..."

"Because I saaaw her today, but she didn't seem ooout of sorts at all."

"Oh, you saw Rika?"

"Yesss, in front of her office. I think she was about to go out driiinking with her coworker... Maaaki, was it? She said she just returned from her faraway faaamily home."

"Maaaki" must have been Maki Shimizu. And that family home

must have been her old place in Kobe. Emi had no idea—and while Rika had no obligation to submit a travel report to Emi, if she was off in Kobe the entire time their current radio silence was unfolding, that worried her.

"Ohhh… Alllso, I'm not sure if I should tell you or not, but she had a message for youuu."

"She did?"

"She told me to tell you, 'I think I can talk calmly about things when a little bit more time has passed.' I don't know what that meeeans, but…"

Emeralda might not have, but to Emi it could only mean one thing.

"…All right."

"Does that have to do with why you don't want to bring this up with herrr?"

"I—I hardly know what anything's got to do with anything any longer."

"Emiliaaa?"

"By next year… Who am I even going to think is important to my life?"

"Well, why worry about next yeeear already? Don't fools rush in where deeemons fear to tread?"

"Angels. Where angels fear to tread. Not that they'd be much of an improvement. But if the demons found out how I'm feeling right now…"

Emi put her head down, arms around her knees.

"I don't know if I could ever recover."

"……"

If she was this far gone, not even Emeralda had any advice for her.

✳

The day after she listened to Emi's pure, simple, unadorned confession, Emeralda sent a tersely worded Idea Link to Albert explaining that she couldn't return yet. Albert was at a total loss for words, of course, but even he understood that Emeralda wouldn't take such a drastic step without a reason. *"Hey,"* he said before he shut off the Link, his voice resigned, *"it's your funeral"*—and as glad as she was that he understood, that little closing remark meant Albert was now crossed off the list of friends to bring souvenirs home to.

Now she was lying on the guest futon next to Emi's bed, thinking over matters in her pajamas despite it being well into the afternoon.

"Hmm... But could Ms. Sasaki really ever be jealous of Emiliaaa? ...Ahh, I suppose just thiiinking about it won't solve the problem..."

She then napped for another hour or so before she finally forced herself up.

"Why don't I just go," she said, "and see for myselllf?"

Looking at the wadded and torn shift schedule stuck on the refrigerator, Emi, Chiho, and Maou were all on the evening shift. "A picture's worth a thouuusand words," she sang to herself as she got dressed, "so time to get a picture of my owwwn!"

There was still time until Chiho's shift began, however. Heading to MgRonald now would likely lead to awkward stares and perhaps a swift boot out the door from Emi. So...

"Sooo I was wondering if I could iiinterview you for a little bit."

"I dunno about what but be my guest."

Half an hour later, she was in Room 101 of Villa Rosa Sasazuka, sharing a *kotatsu* table with Nord and Erone. Nord seemed pretty nonplussed by this sudden self-invite but allowed her in the room nonetheless.

"Hello, Erone!"

"...Hello."

Erone was reading a book—in Japanese. "Ah," explained Nord, "he's been borrowing them from Ms. Shiba or buying them from used bookstores, but these children seem to be picking up on this nation's language without any particular instruction. Here you are."

He offered Emeralda a cup of tea to warm herself a little.

"So what briiings me here today..."

"Hmm?"

"As Emilia's faaather, what sort of…condiiitions are you looking for in her potential husband?"

"………………………Hmm?"

Nord froze, not following the gist of the question.

"No, ah, I don't meeean anything deep by it. I remain siiingle myself, but I figured, as her father, you would want her to be as haaappy as possible before anything else."

"Well, of course…"

"So I was wonnndering what kind of life you'd like Emilia to leeead, going forward."

It was hard to grasp the intent behind that stony smile of hers, but Nord thought over the question, cup in hand.

"…I can't say I have any requests, no."

"Oh? You dooon't?"

"Nope." He put his elbow on the table, hand supporting his head. "Laila and I have already failed to provide a happy life for her, after all. I'm not sure we're too qualified to go up to Emilia's partner and say *you'd better make her happy.*"

"You're worried you aren't quaaalified? It seems like aaany parent would want that, I think."

"That's nice of you to say, Emeralda, but living here, I can't help but think sometimes. Looking at how Emilia ought to live, it sure seems to me that being here in Japan might actually be the best thing."

"And why is thaaat? Not to be too forrrward, but all during our journey, Emilia talked about wanting to work your fiiields with you again."

"Oh, I know. Emilia told me herself. But I've been in Japan for a while by now, and I think I know a thing or two about this nation." He snickered. "Japan… Or this world, really… You won't find any man on this planet stronger than Emilia, will you?"

"……………Well…………" Nord's point-blank response caught Emeralda more than a little off guard. "Perhaps not, no. In mooore ways than onnne."

"And if you think of it that way, I highly doubt Emilia will wind up unhappy, no matter who she marries. Don't you think so?"

"That sounds like quiiite a leap to meee…"

"Her journey gave her a lot of mental toughness, I'd say, and the time she spent here alone must've added to that. I'm sure she would have preferred not to go through that, given the choice, but now that she has, I think she needs to make that a net positive in her life. Besides, Emilia is no fool. She'd never be attracted to some lazy bum without a decent head on his shoulders. So whoever she chooses, I'm not planning to complain about it at all."

"…I see."

"Just out of curiosity, do you think there's someone like that in Emilia's life?"

"Nooo, not yet at least…but if there waaas, I wouldn't be having this conversaaation with you in the first place."

"True enough," Nord said with a hearty laugh.

"So if I could ask you a somewhat more pooointed question…"

"Go ahead. I'll answer it if I can."

"All riiight…" She looked at Nord, expression unchanged. "Do you thiiink Emilia will celebrate Chriiistmas here next year?"

"…" Nord fell silent.

"Christmas?" chimed in Erone. "Acieth mentioned it to me. She made it sound like some kind of food festival?"

Acieth was clearly a bad influence on him. If Amane or Ashiya were here, they'd both be shaking, no doubt.

"Yes," Emeralda replied, the lilt in her voice gone. "Next year, and the next one, and the next one. What do you think, sir?"

"I—I…"

"I'm sure you're aware of what your wife expects of Emilia?"

"…I am," came the somewhat distressed-sounding reply.

"As I've said to you before, I am on Emilia's side. I will support her in any endeavor she desires, just as much as I'm sure Chiho Sasaki would. That is why I sincerely hope she doesn't plunge herself into a battle she doesn't want for herself…even if the rest of the world wants her to."

"……"

For a while, the only sounds to be heard were Emeralda's soft voice, Erone turning the pages in his book, and the light footsteps of someone in Room 201—probably Urushihara—plodding back and forth between the kitchen and the window. It took nearly five minutes for Nord to finally squeeze the words out.

"Lately, you know, sometimes I've seen Laila and Emilia come home together." He turned toward the thin door at the front of Room 101. "I…I don't really hope for anything, because I'm sure I don't know. I don't know what those two women's future should be like or what they want from it."

There was no way Nord wasn't aware of the facts Gabriel presented to Emeralda at that MozzBurger in Nerima. Not someone who loved Laila as much as he did. And that knowledge—the fact that her daughter might be immortal, no matter what she thought about it—put him at a crossroads.

"That day I went to my wife's apartment… I hate to admit it, but all we really did was clean up her place. That night, we went out to eat at this diner in Nerima, but it wasn't until I came back here when I realized it was the first time all three of us shared a meal together. I was so exhausted that I can barely remember what I even ordered."

Nord flashed an odd-looking smile, haunted by both happiness and loneliness.

"But it was such an enjoyable time. I don't know if they'd describe it as such, but…"

"……"

"And I think that's what I want for them. That sort of constant, unchanging routine, the kind where they have trouble remembering what they had for dinner yesterday. I hope that's what they want, too. But before too long, unless something changes, we're going to lose one of the most important pieces for that happiness."

Would that be Emi? Or Laila? Or Nord?

"Emilia already knows what Laila wants."

"?!"

Emeralda gasped at this unimaginable statement. She knew they had grown at least a little closer, but *that* close?

"Now, that's a little different from accepting Laila's request. But like I said, Emilia's been coming home right alongside Laila as of late, when she's done with work. It's not exactly the approach she took with Maou, but in her own way, she's trying to strike a fair stance with Laila. They've been talking to each other a lot the past little while, in this room."

"To each other," he'd said. And not while Nord was gone. Just as Maou demanded Chiho accompany him, Emi and Laila were no doubt asking their father and husband to help arbitrate their discussions.

"Of course, she may listen to all this discussion and flatly refuse her in the end, but…"

Despite Emeralda's initial surprise, this seemed possible to her. And what Nord had heard from those two largely matched up with what Gabriel told Emeralda at MozzBurger.

"I married Laila fully aware she was an angel. I was the one who asked for her hand in marriage."

"Ahh…"

Emeralda tensed up, worried that this would descend into a bunch of lovey-dovey nonsense again.

"She told me she was immortal. That she already wasn't a human being. She told me not to expect children or for her to age alongside me. She cried when she did. But I didn't mind. I loved her from the heart, and she loved me. So if I could be part of her life for at least a little bit, nothing could have made me happier. So I asked her again."

Yep. Just as lovey-dovey as Emeralda thought. He was even holding his chin out a little.

"But when Emilia was born…I'm sure Laila must've been terrified. She had managed to become an Ente Islan, but with her angelic blood, she was worried Emilia would be too different from humans. I didn't hear about that until after the Devil King's Army attacked and Emilia was separated from me. I think we talked about that when we all went to Chofu, a while back? It was just before I went to Japan."

You were all lovey-dovey about her then, too, Emeralda caught herself almost saying. Instead, she just nodded.

"I don't know if immortality is a good thing or not. If my wife and daughter stay young and beautiful long after I die, that might be a wonderful thing. But I'm sure it means they'll have to keep saying good-bye to so many people they love. And being immortal, once they grow sick of living, what's left at the end...?"

Nord deliberately avoided going into detail on that.

"So I just don't know. As her father, I want her to live as long and happy a life as she can. There are so many wonderful things to see in this world, far too many to get to in one life. But the longer you live, the more pain and suffering you have to deal with. That's why I want Emilia to round out her life as a human being—but to achieve that, she may need to wage a battle she has no interest in fighting. If she's sent out there, she might die in combat. If she does, it'll mean I've taken this girl who could've been young and beautiful for all eternity and sent her to her doom. I'd regret it my entire life. So what should I do? What will make Emilia and Laila happy? I just don't know."

"Nord..."

"If I could fight," he continued, the cup almost at the breaking point in his iron grip, "I'd never let Emilia do it. I'd gladly step on the battlefield to protect the future of the world in her place. If I stumble across the secret to immortality along the way, then maybe I could support my wife's and daughter's decisions the way a real father and husband could. But I don't have even a crumb of Emilia's strength. I'm no help to either of them. All I can do is sit here and watch what they decide to do. It's incredibly irritating."

"...I don't know what happiness is, either..."

Erone put his hand over Nord's.

"But what I do know is, both of them know how you feel about them. So stop beating yourself up. You aren't just making Laila and Emilia happy. You're making me happy and Acieth, too."

"Erone..."

"We get to eat our fill every day besides."

"Ha... That is a verrry happy feeling, isn't it? A nice meeeal when you need it."

Emeralda laughed a little at Erone's stone-faced joke.

"I can't choose my way by myself, but I know I'll never forget the happy times I spent with all of you in this city. No matter what Emilia and Laila decide to do, I know that'll always be true. You're not useless to us at all, Nord. You'd never be."

".........Yeah, I sure hope not."

Emeralda had no way to guess how Nord took Erone's words. But using a hand to wipe the tears from his eyes, he turned back toward her.

"If I can't do anything but look on...I guess this is how I would answer it. The first question."

There was nothing contrived about his expression—almost like pure desperation, as if he had already gotten over everything.

"If Emilia's hope is to spend Christmas in Japan next year, I'll do whatever she wants. Dress up as Santa, anything. And that's what I really want—to join her along the way, as much as I can."

"...Thank you. I apologize for the rudeness of my questions."

She couldn't help but say sorry for the way she had tested his heart like that.

◇

Room 101 of Villa Rosa Sasazuka. The mother and daughter still looked a bit awkward, facing each other like this, but in Nord's eyes, their relations had dramatically warmed up since the day they had cleaned out her apartment.

This was where Laila told Emi the story of Ignora discovering the key to immortality as a way to fend off the pandemic affecting her home planet. Emi listened silently, asking not a single question, and in the midst of it, Nord played with Alas Ramus. It was a happy if awkward little space. Laila's story was largely the same as what Gabriel told Chiho and the rest of the gang, but Emi and Nord weren't aware of that at the time.

"The two of them came to that moon-side laboratory as additional staff at first. I was pretty shocked when I saw the photos on their lab IDs. I mean, they looked like children on their way home from school—and when I actually met them, that only cemented the image. It was Sariel who took them there; he was working for the lab's legal department at the time, and the higher-ups supporting the lab trusted him to be their attendant."

"Hmmm..."

These two young researchers were sent up there after the lab spent a year looking for a solution and finding nothing. Their names were Caiel and Sikeena.

"The boy was Caiel, and the girl was Sikeena. And you know, Caiel had silver hair with just a lock of purple at the front."

"Silver and purple?"

"Mm? What is it?"

"What, Mommy?"

Emilia's surprised eyes were pointed at Alas Ramus, having a ball riding on Nord's back.

Laila nodded. "That's right. Caiel was the personification of our planet's Yesod, and Sikeena was the personification of its Malkuth. We didn't know about any of that back then. The lab really looked at them through rose-colored glasses, this pair of fresh college grads sent over by the leaders of our planet. We had been spinning our wheels for a year, and we knew the government wanted results. Things were pretty strained."

But once they were brought on as Ignora's assistants, things progressed quickly.

"We finally found a gene that could resist the pandemic in our experiments with mice... Well, the equivalent lab animal in our world, but you get the idea. Once we did, Caiel and Sikeena began to be treated much, much differently. It was a breakthrough, and Ignora essentially gave them all the credit. That kind of thing usually sparks a lot of jealousy in the research world, but thanks to a certain someone watching over Ignora's group and providing them support in this otherworldly enterprise, there wasn't too much discord."

"A certain someone..." Emi looked up at the ceiling. He hadn't appeared since way back at the start of the story, but by the way Laila phrased this…

"Right. That was Satanael Noie, a talented scientist and Ignora's partner of sorts. A strong sorcerer…and I'm sorry, dear, but a chief researcher I really looked up to at the time."

"Ahh," an unoffended Nord replied as he continued with Alas Ramus's piggyback ride, "I'm sure it happens if you live as long as you have."

Emi worried this could touch off some jealousy, as much as they both enjoyed rambling on without end about their love for each other. Both of them, reassuringly, were too mature for that.

"Ignora was a scientific genius, and she knew it. Satanael, on the other hand, was more about hard work and undaunting effort. He knew full well he wasn't as much of a natural talent as Ignora, and that's why he loved her and her ability so much. He wasn't the kind of person to let that turn into envy and hostility. That made him popular among everybody there, man and woman. I was the new girl in the medical department, so I'd be at Ignora's place all the time delivering medicine and medical equipment, and I got to speak with him a lot. That's a lot of why I felt so much for him."

"If I could just ask, what kind of person was he like?"

"Father…"

Emi shot a look at Nord, who, it turned out, was a lot more interested in bending the subject this way than she thought. Surprisingly, Laila accepted it.

"Oh, that's actually pretty important. He was a very *fair* person. A vastly talented sorcerer. He wasn't completely separated from the real world the way theoretical researchers can often be—he was firmly rooted in reality. But that didn't mean he was this gruff professor type, either. Sometimes, he'd be up all night drinking with friends and looking like a mess the next day at work. And he was strong, too! One time, he engaged in a little battle training with Gabriel in the lab's recreation room. Gabriel was head of security, handpicked from the military ranks, and you wouldn't believe how handily Satanael whipped him. They had ten matches, and Gabriel didn't win one of them. He was livid about it, of course, but you know what Satanael said? He said, 'All I can do is take care of myself, but you protect everyone here. You being here puts people's minds at ease. Me showing that I'm stronger than you would just rock the boat.' That's the kind of person he was."

If Laila—a woman who normally made no effort at all to hide her love for Nord—painted him in such rosy terms, he must have been an incredibly charismatic person indeed. Nord still looked a little unconvinced, but for now he relented.

"But you know, I couldn't help but find it a little strange, too. By which I mean, a while after Caiel and Sikeena joined us, Satanael started arguing with Ignora a great deal more often. For the most part, it was about Caiel and Sikeena, and I think Satanael wanted to keep them away from Ignora. It was funny—he defended them so much at first, too. I asked why later on, and I guess the gene they discovered hadn't been examined by anyone before. There wasn't any literature on it at all. No nation in our world even had the tech to observe this gene before now, he said, and them of all people finding it was a bit...odd."

At the time, Laila assumed it was the result of Ignora's talents combined with that duo's strength. That assumption was shared by everyone else Satanael voiced his concerns with.

"So it ended there, for the most part, and it was then that Ignora's research really began to take off. It was hard even for Satanael to keep up, but Caiel and Sikeena were still right there, next to her. Now everyone was getting a little suspicious. Yes, maybe Ignora could spearhead research too advanced for anyone else to understand, but why were these kids out of college keeping pace with her? Satanael backed off on his complaints—given the urgency, the research always needed to take precedent—but he still had these vague concerns about their origins, their minds, you know. Then one day, he managed to convince Sariel to find out where they came from."

Pretending to take some time off, Satanael went back down to their home planet to learn about Caiel and Sikeena, only to find that their birth records had likely been forged. No accurate records of their origin existed, and every other document related to them—their parents, their dependents, anything that could be used for identification—was forged as well. According to Sariel's investigation, the two of them all but popped into existence under the wing of the powerful government leader who sent them to the moon.

"Can you trust Sariel on this?"

"He may not act like it much, but he takes his work seriously. A pity his…*other* habits cost him so much."

By that, Emi felt it safe to assume the way Sariel acted around women wasn't much different before reaching Earth.

Regardless, Satanael, now fully suspicious of Caiel and Sikeena, returned to the moon lab—only to find something completely unexpected up there.

"Apparently, even Ignora was starting to question the talents of her two assistants. So she gave them a full-body scan, pretending it was just a regular physical. I guess she tried to track the DNA records in their family register, and she discovered it contained genes normally never found in the human race. In fact, those genes included the 'immortality' gene, the one found in the mouse experiments that they assumed also existed in humans. I was a licensed doctor at the time, but I didn't know much about genetic engineering, so the details were a bit over my head. But apparently, the genes in Caiel's and Sikeena's body cells that defined the limits of their metabolism simply didn't function at all."

All living creatures had a given limit to how much their cells could metabolize in their lives, although this limit varied from individual to individual. Once reached, that's the end of your natural life span. That wasn't the only factor, of course, but metabolism is nonetheless considered a key part of one's life span on Earth, with some theorizing that turning off this limit could stave off old age and death.

"Plus, their genes held a strong immunity against all known disease. The biggest surprise for Ignora was that she couldn't find a single potentially cancerous cell across either of their bodies."

"That's not so uncommon, is it? They were young, you said."

"Well, based on our planet's medical knowledge—we're talking ten thousand years ago, keep in mind—the body, due to assorted reasons, always contains at least a few cells that are threatening to become cancerous. As long as your cancer resistance genes are working fine, your immune system will kill and restore those cells in the blink of an eye. If they stop working or some other unusual event happens that causes cancerous cells to spread, that's what you and I mean when we say that someone has cancer."

Emi only became aware of cancer after coming to Japan. Her knowledge of the disease was vague at best.

"Every day, constantly, your body is being damaged by lots of natural elements—ultraviolet rays, reactive oxygen, and so on. But your body's constantly repairing itself, too. Sometimes, a few cells fall through the cracks and begin the preliminary cancer process, and that's not at all unusual. But if the body isn't seeing any cancerous cells *at all*, that's normally unthinkable. It means every cell in your body is perfect, unblemished."

Laila paused.

"Now, this is just how the people on my planet explained it. I can't say if this applies to cancer in Ente Isla or Earth. As far as I know, it's not that different. But anyway, once she discovered Caiel and Sikeena's secret, Ignora carefully compared the differences between their genes and ours—and amazingly, in the course of a single month, she figured out what genetic adjustments were needed to make ours look more like theirs. That's how things were by the time Satanael made it back from his holiday."

Then, for some reason, Ignora's research began to get bogged down again. Why? Because Caiel and Sikeena suddenly disappeared. Everyone was incredibly suspicious, of course, but Ignora didn't really need them any longer. With Satanael assisting, she took a genetic approach to the pandemic once more and reached a certain conclusion.

"Caiel and Sikeena were like us but also *not* like us. In other words, they were kind of like aliens, with DNA that didn't conform to any human being from our planet. But they were definitely there, posing as human. Ignora figured that tracing where they came from would help her dive deeper into her research. Satanael already knew their records had been forged, so the two worked together to investigate them. And then…they found it. On the moon. The thing you could call their parent."

It appeared, at first, to be a gigantic, withered old tree—one rooted on the surface of the moon, where nowhere near enough air existed. Nobody knew why, but even with all the space probes the planet had launched, this somehow managed to escape detection, despite being located toward the rear of the laboratory's territory. No scans from orbit picked up on it or any other useful underground resources, so developers simply ignored the whole patch of moonscape.

"Ignora only found that tree thanks to a holy energy scan. There was this one intense blip of energy in an otherwise barren space. That's where the tree was, in one of several of these blips on the dark side of the moon. Wells of holy energy, if you will. You see what I'm getting at? That was the Tree of Sephirot for our world, the parent of the Sephirah and the 'mother' of Caiel and Sikeena."

Taking a sample from the tree, Ignora ran a DNA check and found it matched Caiel and Sikeena perfectly. They were gone, but the tree provided all the experimental samples they needed. It helped her and Satanael's research advance by leaps and bounds every day.

"Now, if I can change the subject for a moment… Satanael kind of had a thing for Ignora. He loved her talents, and he deeply loved her personality. I kept my own emotions in check really, because it was so obvious that he would get in the way of anything…further I'd have for her. But after Caiel and Sikeena disappeared, it took a mere five years for the immortality gene to be completed. They were close in their research the whole time, but they were close as people, too.

And on the day they formally established the genetic process and ushered in an era of immortality, where nobody had to worry about disease again...they got married."

"Uh?" Even Emi had to give this a bewildered grunt. "B-but wait, if Ignora is Lucifer's mother, then are you saying Satanael... The Devil Overlord Satan of old... Whaaa?!"

Laila nodded at her daughter's most dramatic reaction of the day.

"That's what I'm saying. Satanael Noie is Lucifer's father."

THE DEVIL KING IS OUT OF THE OFFICE (3)

After Emeralda left Room 101 with a much better understanding of Nord's feelings, she headed over to the MgRonald by Hatagaya station, back on her original objective—observing Emi and Chiho at work. It was her first visit since their combined birthday party, but luckily she still remembered the way there.

It was evening, and the sky was already starting to turn red by the time Emeralda spotted Chiho sweeping the walkway in front of the entrance.

"Oh? Emeralda? Are you here to have dinner?!"

She greeted her with a smile as she ran up to her. There wasn't a trace of jealousy nor any other dark emotion on her face—and Emeralda noticed she was wearing the Santa hat Emi mentioned.

"Did Yusa know you were coming?"

"Nooo, I didn't saaay anything."

"Ooh, I bet she'll be really surprised! Here, come on in! It's cold out here!"

Stepping inside, the entire staff was in Santa hats, just as promised. It certainly made for a festive atmosphere, although it didn't change much else.

"Do you know how to order and stuff?" Chiho asked, unsure if Emeralda was up on Japan's fast-food culture.

"I think I'll be fiiine. If I mess up, I'll just pretend to be a forrreigner and ask for help. Certainly a lot of decoraaations up, aren't there?"

"Oh, yes! We put up all our Christmas stuff today. I've never worked here when it was like this, so I was kinda looking forward to it. Um, I need to get back to work for now but enjoy your dinner!"

"Keep up the good worrrk," Emeralda replied as Chiho took her dustpan and broom back outside. Then she got in line in front of the register, head swiveling around as she took in all the unusual sights. She spotted Emi a bit beyond the counter, talking to someone with some strange machine attached to her ear. Kisaki, the manager, was also recognizable as the tall woman working upstairs.

With the lines backed up, Chiho opened another register to work through the backlog, winking at Emeralda as she did.

"...Hmmm?"

As she waited for her turn, Emeralda noticed something odd. The number of people working didn't match the total written in Emi's schedule. It wasn't like she had spotted everybody on duty yet, but even she could tell someone was missing.

"Wherrre's the Devil King?" she whispered to Chiho once she reached the register.

"Maou is out training today again," she whispered back. "He'll be back later."

Come to think of it, Emi had mentioned that Maou was busy with that stuff yesterday. Emeralda briskly completed her order with Chiho's support, but they needed to cook up a new batch of fries, so she took her seat with a burger, a drink, and a number card. Off in the kitchen space, she saw Chiho calling for Emi. Their conversation seemed like nothing unusual from Emeralda's perspective; maybe they were getting along better than Emi feared.

In the end, it was Emi who delivered Emeralda's fresh-cooked fries to her.

"What brings you here?" she asked, keeping an eye out for any nosy customers nearby.

"Ohhh, you were all worked up yesterday, so I was kind of concerrrned..."

"…You liar. You just wanna gawk at us all."

"I will not denyyy thaaat," Emeralda replied, grinning wryly. "But I can't do that if the Devvvil King isn't here. I heard he was in traaaining, but what kind of training is it? I thought he was already the main forrrce running this place."

"…Oh, I guess I didn't mention it. He's training to become a full-time employee, so he's been gone practically every day lately. I guess he's gonna be salaried before too long."

"Salaried…? Whaaa?!" Emeralda half jumped out of her seat. "So the Devil King wants to pursue life as a laaaborer in this world?!"

"That's always been his goal, I guess, so none of the demons were too surprised by it. Yesterday, he was going around with Ms. Kisaki in this business suit that looked *so* bad on him, but today he's out alone, visiting a MgRonald with a different configuration from this one."

Deliveries and MgCafés were far from the only unique things a MgRonald location could potentially boast. There were Mini-Mags, located inside supermarkets, big-box stores, and food courts with a common shared seating space. There were drive-thru MgRonalds, mostly along national highways. There were locations inside amusement parks and such, open limited hours and subject to different operational rules.

"If he goes full-time, there's no predicting what kind of store he'll be assigned to, so he's going around all the different offices and locations to build up experience and stuff."

"Wow. So maaaybe it won't be long before he's managing this restaurant, huh?"

"I don't know if it'll be this one. But it won't come that easy."

It went without saying that only the most talented of crewmembers got a chance to undergo full-time training. However, that didn't necessarily result in a permanent position, either. It wasn't the way most people went up the MgRonald ranks, and while not even Kisaki as a manager knew how it fully worked, there were cases in the past where people trained for nearly a year while part-timing and still didn't get offered a full-time spot.

"Well, the Devil Kiiing never liked Laila to staaart with, so I doubt he'll take her request nowww, huh? He has a goooal he's working hard for, and now he's about to achieeeve it."

"................Maybe."

That reply sounded incredibly noncommittal.

"Sorry, I need to go back to work."

"Of—of courrrse! Sorry to get in the waaay!"

"It's fine. Take your time… Thank you for calling MgRonald by Hatagaya station. My name is Yusa, and I'm ready to…"

The moment she stepped away, she pushed that machine back into her ear, talking with someone. Emeralda watched her go about her business for a while, until Chiho approached. "What did you think of your meal?" she asked. "That's a special winter season set. It wasn't available at the birthday party."

"Oh, it was verrry good! But I would probably gain weiiight if I ate it every day, wouldn't I?"

"Ha-ha-ha! I'm sure you would."

"Emilia was telling me the Devil Kiiing has a lot on his plaaate right now."

"Oh, you heard about his training? Yeah, he's been working here this whole time so he could nail that opportunity. Whenever he shows up here these days, he's got this crazy resolute look on his face."

"Reeeally?"

"Yeah. He's in, like, super high spirits. I worry every time that Yusa will pick a fight with him about it, but—you know—I think she's kinda rooting for him, too."

"Hmm. That's a little uuunexpected."

"Well, lately, who can say? They sure aren't at each other's throats like they were before they came back from Ente Isla."

For a moment, Emeralda recalled Emi's concern. At the very least, Chiho, from her vantage point below her, didn't seem to exude even the slightest shred of envy.

"But since Maou's been so busy, we haven't been able to all eat dinner together in Room 201 the way we normally do, which is kind of a pity. I was hoping we could use this as an opportunity to all get friendlier with one another, but it's proving kinda hard to work out."

Hearing this, Emeralda decided to ask a somewhat malicious question.

"But if Emilia and the Devil King get a little toooo friendly with each other, you know, they might get maaarried and raise Alas Raaamus together, hmm?"

Would she freak out? Would she snap back at her? Would she deny it? For Chiho, the answer was none of the above.

"Mmm, I don't think I'm losing out personally…but if it happens, it happens, I guess."

Emeralda looked back blankly. Chiho responded by looking as bold as possible, nostrils flared.

"But I'm not just gonna sit there wringing my hands! If it comes to it, whether it's a Hero with a holy sword or a Great Demon General, I'm ready to fight back with everything I got!"

"Uhh…hmmm?"

Before Emeralda could figure out which Great Demon General she meant…

"Besides, I love Maou *and* Emi a lot, so no matter what happens, I'm confident we'll all stay friends!"

There wasn't a single dark cloud to this ringing declaration. It was clear this was Chiho's true emotion coming out. In other words, Emi had nothing to worry about.

"There's no beating youuu, no…"

Emeralda began to feel like such a petty woman for prodding this young woman like that. Relenting on that front, she instead whispered about some other business of hers—something she didn't intend to handle here.

"I'd like to discuss something eeelse with you later on…"

It was about planning a Christmas party for Alas Ramus, a topic that instantly made Chiho's eyes light up. They agreed to head for

Devil's Castle after work, where they'd try to win over Ashiya and the gang.

The two of them arrived at Room 201 at around six in the evening.

"A Christmas party? Why the heck would you come up with something ridiculous like that?"

Urushihara's whining was summarily ignored by the rest of Room 201.

"That's a great idea, Emeralda! Alas Ramus has been working just as hard as Yusa, hasn't she?"

"Could I ask you to help me handle the decorations?" Suzuno asked Chiho. "I have ample time at hand, so if we need to purchase anything, leave it to me."

"If it is for Alas Ramus's sake," Ashiya reflected, "so be it."

"Thank you sooo much, everyonnne. I knew you'd see it my way!"

"*I* didn't agree with you! Hey! Hey..."

With even Ashiya signing on for it, Urushihara felt obliged to be the lone voice of dissent on the matter, as pointless as he knew it'd be.

"But no matter the size, location will be an issue." Ashiya looked around the room. "If we are to hold this for Alas Ramus, there will no doubt be more people invited. Our own apartment will not be enough space."

Room 201 was the kind of place that needed only seven people—Maou, Ashiya, Urushihara, Emi, Chiho, Suzuno, and Alas Ramus—to get packed to the gills. That didn't include party planner Emeralda, Alas Ramus's little sister Acieth, Acieth's semi-adopted brother Erone, and Amane and Nord, always accompanying Acieth and Erone when they were together. With all of them, there'd be no room to breathe, and this wasn't just a gathering of people, either. As a Christmas party, there'd be more food on the table, not to mention the decorations Suzuno mentioned.

"We cannot hold it at MgRonald, I suppose, like we did with Emilia and Ms. Sasaki's party. What do you think?"

"Yeees, Bell, about that…" Emeralda shot an eye toward Ashiya and Urushihara. "I think Emiiillia's apartment would be niiice."

"…What?"

"Okay, uh, I'm not going."

"Urushihara!"

The offer made Ashiya's eyebrows clamp down and Urushihara get even more bratty.

"Bell, have you and Sasaki seen Emilia's plaaace?"

"I have. It should be able to hold all of us. But what does Emilia think?"

"I haven't aaasked her yet. We can't have all of us together on the twenty-fourth or twenty-fifth aaanyway, and we can't do this without the Devvvil King, so…"

"Hmm… I doubt my liege would say no if it is for Alas Ramus's sake, but holding it at Emilia's residence…?" Ashiya's eyebrows quirked up, as if just realizing something. "Thinking about it, neither I, nor Urushihara, nor probably my liege himself knows where the Hero lives."

"Huh?"

It was Chiho who lobbed that surprised gasp. Suzuno, already made aware of this by Emi, sat silently and watched how things unfolded.

"None of you demons know it?"

"I am aware it is an apartment in Eifukucho, of course. But I just now realized that I do not know the address. I do not think I have even seen it."

"You've never been there before?!"

"Why would Maou need to go there, dude? It's usually her coming in here, beating up on all of us, then leaving."

"Well, yes, but…"

Chiho had to accept that Urushihara's point-blank assertion was on the mark.

"I doubt Emilia has ever had any interest in inviting us over," added Ashiya. "And we did not have free rein over demonic power at the time. If we tried tracking down and invading the Hero's home, she might have defeated us right then and there."

It was easy to forget given their current friendlier relations, but Maou and Emi were supposed to be mortal enemies. It surprised Chiho a little.

"But regardless," he continued, "if we used Emilia Justina's apartment, I doubt she would want us over. However, I also doubt Alas Ramus would be willing to participate if my liege was not in attendance. Perhaps we should consider another site?"

"I appreciate your concerrrn, but I have another reeeason for wanting to borrow her space. I think at least one person will attend precisely becaaause we hold it in there."

"In there? You mean Laila?"

"Yeees, her exaaactly," Emeralda said, nodding at Chiho. "I think, with recent eveeents, Emilia and Laila are a bit closer than befooore. But giiiven that, I think it's important to show Laila that her scheeeme isn't going to be accepted thaaat easily by them…"

"Meaning that Emilia will use teaching Alas Ramus about Christmas as a sign that she'd prefer to take root here in Japan?"

The day she had run into Rika and Maki, Emeralda had been seriously concerned that there wouldn't be a next year. She didn't want Emi to accept Laila's request at all.

"I apologize if this is immodest to aaask, but do any of you—Alciel, and Luciferrr, and Ms. Sasaki, and Bell—do aaany of you think Emilia and the Devil Kiiing should take Laila's offer?"

The four of them exchanged glances for a moment.

"Alciel and Luciferrr, you listened to Laila in this room, and I thiiink you know what Gabriel told us about, too. And the more I heeear, the less I feel Emilia and her cohorts need to lend a haaand at all…"

"Well, yeah… I mean, dude, as someone who was there at the time, it's like, hey, do whatcha want. If Maou's up for it, that's a different story, but…"

"Even if His Demonic Highness says yes, I am still against it. Right now is a vital time in my liege's career. If he creates yet more work for himself and shuts away his future as Devil King, everything would go to waste."

"I agree," Suzuno added. "I want to respect their choices, but I see so little good faith on the other side of the equation."

"Yeah," said Chiho. "Like I told Urushihara earlier, maybe I feel some sympathy for the angels' past, but I think Gabriel and everyone are being way too unreasonable."

"Indeeed." Emeralda beamed victoriously. "I think Emilia and Laila growing cloooser is a different discussion from Emilia listening to her taaale. Emilia has so many people who cherrrish her. There's so much in Japan and Ente Isla she holds as precious. I think we need to show Laila that it won't be easy to convince her otherwiiise."

"Yeah, but that's just Emilia, right? What about Maou, dudette?"

"He is traaaining so he can become more strongly connected with Japaaan, isn't he? I doubt he needs any more conviiincing to turn down Laila by now."

Chiho and Ashiya both nodded.

"Yeah…"

"True enough."

"And I knowww we are kind of taking advaaantage, but I can think of another invitee who will be an equally great help if we hold it in Emiiilia's place."

"You mean…"

Emeralda nodded before Suzuno could guess. "Maki might be difficult, ignorant as she is of the situaaation, but wouldn't Rika be interested in attending?"

"… "

Chiho's and Ashiya's faces tensed up. Urushihara and Suzuno picked up on it.

"I think Laila should knowww that Ms. Sasaki isn't the onnnly friend Emilia holds dear in this country, no?"

Emeralda pleaded her case, unsure how to read this nervousness on their part.

"I know this might be a paaain for you demons, but if you'll agree to this paaarty, I'd like to hold it in Emilia's apartment. I'd be happy to cover all the costs apart from Alas Ramus's giiifts, and I'll persuade Emilia to agree to it, toooo."

"Well, my gal, if you'll cover for it, then it's all up to what Maou thinks, huh?" Urushihara turned toward Ashiya, trying to gauge his opinion. Ashiya kept his stony look on his face.

"My liege is already an extremely busy man. Whether he agrees to it or not, I cannot say whether he is able to participate."

"Oh, I knowww. It all comes down to whether Daddy is up for it. We can work out the other arraaangements later."

It was a very Japanese way of arranging things—making sure the patriarch was around for it, despite the long hours he spent at work.

Soon, Emeralda bowed at Ashiya and left Room 201. Chiho spent the next little while half cajoling the unenthusiastic Ashiya and Urushihara and half chatting about Maou's work before realizing how late it was getting.

"Well, I better get home myself."

"Oh, are you leaving? Would you like to have dinner?"

"Thanks, but I didn't tell my mom I'd eat here, so I need to get back… Urushihara, if Maou says yes, you better show up, too!"

"I'll, uh, do my best?" he blankly offered back.

"Ms. Sasaki?" Ashiya said as Chiho put her shoes on by the front door.

"Hmm?"

"Let me walk you home. I have some shopping to do anyway."

"Oh? Um, sure."

She had walked home alone fairly often lately, there being no particular threat to her life to speak of—but even discounting that, Ashiya's offer seemed a bit sudden. Before she could say yes, he was already grabbing the ultralight down jacket hanging off a drawer handle and walking out the door behind her.

"…I apologize," he said the moment they were off apartment grounds. "My walking you home and shopping were, ah, just excuses."

"I thought as much, yeah."

It wasn't a surprise to Chiho. She figured there must be a reason for Ashiya's uncharacteristically pushy behavior.

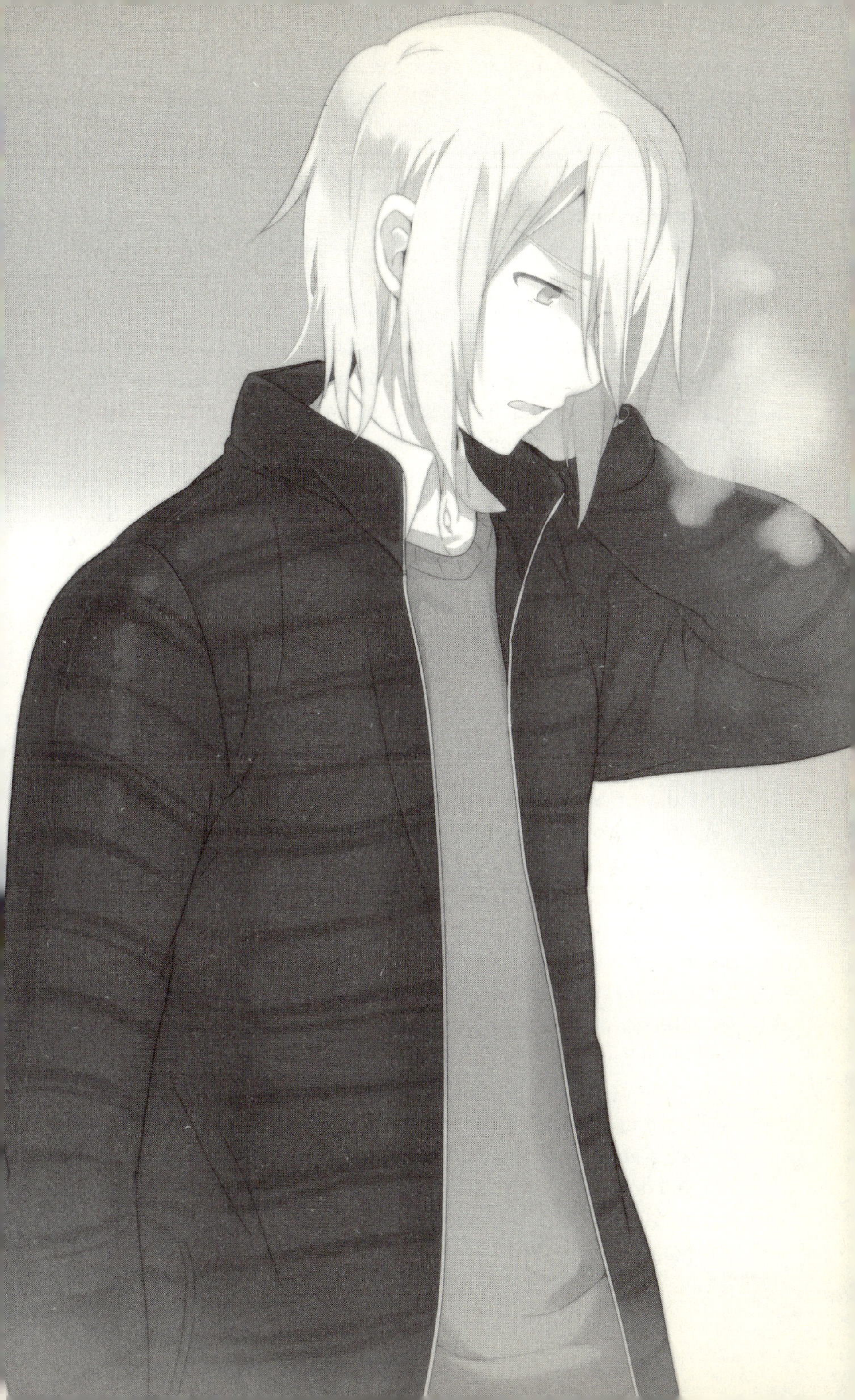

"Ah, but I will gladly walk you home, however, and I do have an item or two to pick up, so I did not intend to lie to you. But, er…"

"Is this about Rika?"

"…It is," he admitted, walking a step behind Chiho. "Have you met her before?"

"Yes," she replied, "on the same day you did."

"I see." He nodded, looking more hesitant than Chiho had ever seen him before. "It makes sense, then. Emilia seemed entirely unaware."

His voice indicated to her that, if Emi were to find out what Ashiya did to Rika, he feared she'd react aggressively to it.

"I don't think Rika's said anything to her. She told me she didn't feel she could, really."

"Ah…" Ashiya took a deep breath and fished his brand-new smartphone out of his pocket. "I apologize," he said, choosing his words carefully for reasons Chiho couldn't fathom. "I suppose Ms. Suzuki's been forced to…look out for us in the Devil King's Army. For our weaknesses."

"Hee-hee-hee! You say that," Chiho replied in a deliberately cheerful voice, "but it's that weakness that attracts us all to you. Not that I want you weak forever, of course. On that front, at least as far as I can tell, you're still a lot more sincere than Maou is."

Ashiya looked down at her, a little surprised, then broke into a grin. "I suppose I have no right to chastise my liege. Honestly…"

Sasazuka station and the Jizo Street shopping center next to it were now in full-on Christmas mode. The flashy lights and decorations looked like something from a different world.

"I thought the whole human race was this disposable thing."

Chiho wasn't sure she had ever heard Ashiya let out such an unbelievably human sigh before. It was the first time Ashiya had ever sighed about anything he had done in the past.

"I have no regrets…but I still cannot get it off my mind. I keep worrying about how she has been since."

"Oh, I don't think Rika's the type of woman to break down in tears just because her crush turned her down."

"That is exactly why I am concerned. About…assorted things."

Ashiya turned his eyes toward Chiho. He was absolutely right, and Chiho understood that all too well—but it was nothing either of them could solve just by thinking about it. So she decided to turn the topic toward something more accessible.

"Would you like me to talk to Maou about holding the Christmas party at Emi's place?"

"No, I think it best if I bring it up, so everyone in the Devil King's Army is on the same page as quickly as possible. You heard what Emeralda Etuva said."

"All right. Maybe that's for the better, yeah. Maou hasn't really been at MgRonald when I'm there. Now that I think about it, we haven't seen each other in a little while."

"No? I suppose going full-time makes things more difficult, yes."

They continued to casually chat about Maou and the restaurant. Before long, they were at Chiho's door.

"Well, thank you for joining me. And if we do hold that party, you're invited, of course."

"I…"

"This might be kind of impertinent of me to say, Ashiya…"

"Hmm?"

"But I feel like both you and Rika are making a big mistake. I wasn't there to see it, of course, but looking at you, I'm pretty sure about that."

"Ah…"

Chiho gave him a big smile. "You really can't chide Maou right now, I don't think. Because maybe you think you've given an answer, but really you haven't."

"Huh?!"

"And with that, thanks again. See you later!"

Leaving that epic riddle for the utterly confused Ashiya to ponder over, she went inside.

"I haven't…?"

Too serious-minded to understand what she meant, he went back home to the apartment—and immediately back out again to do the shopping he forgot about.

＊

"Hmm… I don't know if I'll be able to make my own. I need to think about what we do with them afterward…"

The next day, back on the clock, Chiho gave a questioning look to the Christmas decorations dotted around the dining space.

"What's up, Chi? Something about the decorations bothering you?"

"Oh! Ms. Kisaki!"

Mayumi Kisaki, the manager, gave Chiho a curious look as she pointed at the golden tinsel right above their heads.

"Is it falling down?"

"No, I was just using some free time to think a bit about what makes for good Christmas decorations…"

"You should be using that free time to find work to do," Kisaki quipped, putting a hand to her hip for emphasis.

"Oh, um, sorry."

"So did any of the decorations look off to you when you did your rounds?"

"…No, ma'am."

"Good. Back to work, then. Marko's not here today, so we're a man down this shift. It's gonna be a packed dinner rush, so hang in there."

"Okay!"

Chiho followed her behind the counter, thankful that Kisaki didn't gripe at her further about being idle.

"Where's Mr. Maou today, by the way?"

"A MgRonald managed by a friend of mine. Different configuration but Marko's already been there a few times, so today's training ought to go pretty smoothly."

"The one at Fushima-en?"

"Oh, you know it?"

The Mag at the Fushima-en theme park had enlisted Maou to fill in on several occasions before.

"MgRonald locations in theme parks during the season are pretty unique setups. The way I hear it, they're always a part of the cycle during training periods like this."

"The way you hear it? Don't they tell you about the training schedule in advance?"

"..."

Kisaki paused, taking a quick look around the dining space. "This isn't something I learned until I sent Marko off to training," she solemnly replied, "but even if you undergo the full-time training, the chances of you becoming a salaried employee aren't actually that high."

"Really?"

"Only HR and the main office know what happens in training. Now that we're past the initial portion where I'm accompanying him around, the managers like me only get told when a trainee's coming, and that's about it. Mizushima, my friend at the Fushima-en location, would normally be able to give him some inside advice along those lines, but there are so many home-office people involved right now that I doubt she'll be able to."

Kisaki looked down for a moment, deep in thought.

"I think Marko's a great crewmember. But the way the office manager put it to me, great crewmembers aren't always the kind of people that pass this training. I don't really know what standards they're looking for myself. I believe in Marko, of course, and I want him to try his best at it..." She took off her hat and mike for a moment, adjusting them. "But part of me kind of wants to show him a bigger world than this, you know...?"

"Ms. Kisaki?"

"...Ah, never mind. Now we're really getting into nonwork-related topics."

With that wavering statement, Kisaki returned to work.

"Weird," Chiho said to herself. "It's not like she doesn't want Maou to be a full-timer, but..."

Kisaki knew full well how driven Maou was to earn that position.

But the way she put it just now, the idea of Maou continuing up the MgRonald career track seemed to give her genuine concern.

The dinner rush was exactly as hectic as Kisaki said it'd be, with Chiho barely having a moment to breathe until her shift ended at ten in the evening.

"Oh, you getting off now, Chiho?" Emilia asked.

"Yeah. Sorry to leave you, Yusa."

Despite sharing most of her shift with Emi today, the two of them engaged in almost no conversation. Only when Chiho was seated in the break room, trying to gather up the energy to change out of her uniform, did Emi have a chance to chat a bit.

"Sure was crowded today, huh?"

"You said it," Emi replied. "And it's like every single delivery today's on the far edge of our radius, too. I think Kawata's been out driving in the cold all day, poor guy."

"Yeah, he said working outside is pretty easy once you get used to it, but not in this weather, I bet."

"Totally. And I don't really see the point of the Christmas tree sticker on his helmet, either."

These MgRonald-logo holiday stickers, sent from the main office, looked quite literally tacked on. Kisaki was griping about them earlier, too.

"Oh, speaking of that, was Ms. Kisaki talking to you about decorations?"

"You saw that?" Chiho stood up and pointed at the Christmas tree drawn on the break room calendar. "I was just looking at the decorations, figuring out what kind we should get. Looking back, I kinda stopped paying attention to them once I stopped being a kid."

"Ohh, I see. I bet Eme reminded you of them, huh?"

"Yeah."

Emi smiled and took Chiho's hand. "I'm sorry. I know Eme's super gung ho about this."

"Oh, no! I'm really looking forward to it. We don't get to all eat together so much lately, and I dunno if Emeralda told you or not, but it's kind of turning into a rally for our cause. It's really exciting."

"A rally?"

That sounded hyperbolic to Emi at first, until she realized what Chiho meant.

"Ohh, right, is that why Eme wanted to invited Laila and Rika?"

"Yep! We're not gonna let go of our friends that easy!"

Chiho was aflame with enthusiasm. It was almost too bright for Emi to look at.

"So I thought I'd go out and do some handmade decorations and stuff, but it's a little different from making stuff for the Tanabata festival."

"Maybe. It's not like we're gonna go climb up a mountain and chop a tree down or anything."

"Right. And things like tinsel and tree ornaments—I'd have no idea how to make those myself anyway, so we're gonna need to invest a little bit of money, I think."

"Do we really need to go all the way like that...?"

"Totally! We can't take it easy on this if we want Alas Ramus to enjoy Christmas!" Now Chiho was burning even brighter. "But I don't wanna go too far, of course, or I really will wind up like Maou after Tanabata. So I was just thinking that I'd need to discuss it with someone if we're gonna spend money on it, and then Ms. Kisaki showed up."

She smiled awkwardly at Emi. Emi smiled back.

"Yeah, Tanabata was pretty rough..."

Not long after Suzuno came to Japan, Maou picked up a little bamboo decoration to celebrate the Tanabata festival in July from a regular customer who lived nearby. He decorated the MgRonald with it, and between that and the other crew-crafted decorations, the setup really wowed all the midsummer customers. But then Tanabata ended. This was a living bamboo plant, so they couldn't just abandon it. They allowed customers to snip off pieces of it before the festival ended, but most of the bamboo grass was still there after it was all over, so Maou wound up bringing it back to the apartment. He couldn't put it out with the garbage—the guy who gave it to him might notice—so it just sat on the outer corridor for a few days, getting in everyone's way. It eventually withered up despite Maou's best efforts, so he was forced to dispose of it in piecemeal fashion with the rest of the household trash over several days.

"I don't know what drives the Devil King to do stuff like that."

"Huh?"

"Like, is that good for the company, him playing it by ear like that?"

"How do you mean?"

"Well, customers usually like the stuff he does, right? He owes a lot to Kisaki for letting him do it, of course, but..."

"Yeah..."

Emi sat down across from Chiho, her face serious. "But in a business like MgRonald, what people want the most is, you know, this homogeneous package, right? And the Devil King's bamboo stuff was pretty off script."

"Oh."

Chiho recalled back when the MgCafé space first opened in the Hatagaya station location. The coffee clearly tasted different depending on whether Kisaki or Maou made it. Chiho didn't see what the fuss was—if the coffee's good, the coffee's good—but as Maou put it, if Kisaki wasn't around, he'd be forced to give customers what he knew was an inferior product.

"And you know what? I had a customer tell me the other day that Ms. Kisaki's coffee is going down in quality."

"Really?!"

This was a shock to Chiho. There was no way Kisaki, of all people, would slack off on the job. Did this mean...?

"Right." Emi nodded. "It didn't get worse; it had just gotten normal. On script. Akiko heard the same rumors I did about it. It was kind of funny, but..."

"Ms. Kisaki was trying to keep it homogeneous, too...?"

"That's what I'm thinking. I mean, I don't know for sure. It's not really something I can ask her point-blank. But looking back at Tanabata and how Maou handles his customers, I think he's been able to get away with a lot of it because he's got Kisaki watching out for him."

The fact was that quite a few trainees never got a full-time job offer. And between Kisaki's ramblings, the "normal" coffee, and Maou's "nonhomogeneous" workplace habits, perhaps there were more obstacles to Maou's career efforts than Chiho thought. The company had its own vision of how to maximize profits, and there were standards behind that vision, which couldn't be quantified in monetary figures. To put it another way, MgRonald wanted to build a trust with customers, and that trust couldn't go too far above or below the norms that had been established over time. Maou and Kisaki's work was going above and beyond these norms, and it could even be affecting people's trust in the other MgRonalds around them. Being able to provide better service, but deliberately avoiding doing so, might seem terribly unfair at first glance. But if you don't put an upper limit in place, you might find people who inadvertently destroyed that trust and made things worse for others.

To Chiho, Maou pursuing a full-time job was directly correlated with him and Emi staying close to her for the foreseeable future. This new realization put a pall over her heart. Realizing this, Emi felt obligated to say something.

"You know, I want him to keep trying. I don't want him to give up."

"Oh?"

Chiho gave her an astonished look. It wasn't like Emi to voice her support so clearly like that.

"I mean," Emi replied with a nod, "if he gets that job, then he can stay devoted to that, Ente Isla can fully rebuild itself, and we'll never have to worry about him invading or doing anything else stupid ever again."

"Yusa..."

"And you know, sometimes I come over to his place with Alas Ramus to check up on him. Seeing if he's doing anything dumb, I guess you could say. And every time I do... You know, I really want to be around next year. I want to celebrate Tanabata and Christmas again, with you, and Alas Ramus, and everyone else I hold dear. I mean..."

She stood up and headed toward her locker.

"I'm sick of living in this kill-or-be-killed world. So I've decided. I'm sorry, but we're gonna have to make Alciel cry—in two different ways. First, he'll be weeping for joy when Maou gets that job, and then he'll be wailing when he realizes the demons will never get to take over our world."

"...! S-so you'll...!" Chiho half leaped out of her folding chair and embraced the still-changing Emi from behind. "You'll do it, Yusa! You'll really do it!"

"......I can't beat you, Chiho. It's all happening just the way you want it. It drives me nuts."

Her voice grew softer, her face still turned away.

"I...I'm not going to fight anymore."

◇

Marveling at the sight of Chiho and the rest of the group giving him astonished looks, Gabriel picked up where he left off about Ignora, Satanael, and Lucifer.

"Yeah, so Lucifer was born after we left our home planet, after Ignora found a way to make ourselves immortal. But it was still in the experimental stage at that point—kind of like, *we're pretty sure we can do it*, know what I mean? You won't *really* know if you're invincible against disease or old age until at least a few years pass. But anyway, the lab found a way to deal with the pandemic, and the whole world was freakin' out big-time about that. And then, like I told ya at the start, people got into fights over the tech, and it pretty much ruined our planet."

"W-wait a moment! You are abridging yourself far too much!" Suzuno protested.

"Yes, I'm well awaaare that the discovery triggered a waaar, but what about it was enough to destroy the entire plaaanet?" Emeralda added.

"And besides, that doesn't explain how you wound up on Ente Isla's moon!" Chiho exclaimed.

Gabriel raised both hands to quiet his guests. "Chill, chill, chill! There were a lotta reasons for it, all right? But just like Crestia Bell said a second ago, there's nothing particularly surprising or noble about any of it. It's just a cavalcade of terrible events that proved just how stupid the human race really is."

When the pandemic first took root, the first nations to fall were the economically disadvantaged ones, with less of a developed military. Their populations weren't wiped out by the disease, but it did decimate their numbers enough that they couldn't continue as a going concern. As small as these nations were, their downfall wasn't something the world economy was prepared to absorb. The larger powers scrambled to preserve their own finances, and as Ignora and her team continued their research, tensions across borders rapidly approached the breaking point.

Once word got out that the lunar lab's work might provide a solution to the disease, many nations sent people and money to the facility, in hopes of reaping the benefits ahead of anyone else. The lunar base itself was a melting pot of sorts, with Ignora, Satanael, Camael, Raguel, Gabriel, Sariel, and Laila all from different nations, but they had grouped together to try to save the planet.

Once the day came when Ignora's results were formally announced, their home planet began to crack along its national borders. Her country attempted to summon her back home, as did Satanael's. Anyone even slightly involved with the immortality research received similar orders. But from the researchers' point of view, their work had only just begun; it wasn't anything they could put to practical use yet, so going home right now was unthinkable. Satanael and Sariel served as their representatives, trying their best to negotiate with each nation, but their efforts failed to bear fruit.

In fact, the world began to lodge all kinds of shortsighted accusations at the international group formed to manage the lunar base. All sorts of loony stories started going around—researchers being held against their will on the moon, spies being sent to kidnap team members, countries laying claims to the spaceport that all the lab's goods went through. Everyone wanted the immortality formula, no matter how foolish their efforts made them look.

Some nations even tried to duplicate the research themselves, using the information released by the facility and moon colony to the press as a guide. This led to acts of terrorism, carried out by people who believed that one nation hoarding its research was a crime against humanity. This research was supposed to save the world; instead, it plunged the world into chaos—and the pandemic kept spreading the entire time.

The harmful particles in the air that had covered Gabriel's home planet triggered several symptoms at the same time, in multiple areas of the body at once. If someone caught it, unless the victim was very lucky, there was no saving them. Once these particles made their way in through the respiratory organs, they blocked both the body's digestive functions and the nervous system's ability to send and receive signals. If they struck the lungs, they would drastically impact the victim's breathing ability; if they got into the blood, they would turn into a substance that caused blockages and cardiac issues.

This disease struck people in different ways. Some could live out their entire natural lives without being affected, while others would present multiple symptoms after a single, tiny exposure. Most traditional medical approaches were quickly exhausted. All in all, over 30 percent of the population caught this disease, and given that it killed over half its victims within five years, the effects on the world's average life span and population were devastating. By the time the immortality research began to look like the "real thing," so to speak, the human race was willing to fight to the death with one another for even an incomplete version of the findings.

Leaving the planet wasn't an option. Colonies on the moon and elsewhere were accessible only to the highest reaches of society, and there was no guarantee that the harmful particles littered across the star system wouldn't get you there, too. The disease even took a few people in Ignora's laboratory, forcing Gabriel to sound the hazard alarm multiple times.

Even so, these were still the good old days—back when the rule of law still prevailed among the larger nations.

The lunar researchers did their best, finding ways to extend the deadline on their return home while advancing their immortality research. However, the lab was facing more and more obstacles that had nothing to do with academic or technical issues. As chief of security, Gabriel was faced with the grim task of shifting the directive for his personnel from controlling outside threats to actively fighting them off.

Still, Ignora, Satanael, Laila, Camael, and everyone else involved with the research worked tirelessly on, believing that all this strife would come to an end once their job was complete. Facing up to the threat of kidnapping or attacks from foreign nations—or even worse, their own—they went over to the giant tree on the moon to gather samples many times, figuring out not only how to become immortal but how to mass-produce the miracle. In the midst of this storm—none of it their fault—their only support was their fervent desire to save the human race.

Then one day, it happened: Gabriel learned about it from Laila first—Ignora and Satanael were engaged in a heated argument.

"This child is the greatest hope the human race has," Satanael shouted. "The dawn of a new age, one that will bring the light of new dreams to our imperiled future!"

Ignora refused to back down. "But it's complete! It's finally completed! I've done it! We can save the world now!"

As out of the loop as he was, Gabriel knew what this meant. Immortality was near.

Then all of a sudden, a warning alarm sounded off across the entire facility. Gabriel sent a message out asking what was up; he was greeted by the screams of the dying.

"And y'know what they said? 'It's Caiel and Sikeena! They're here! They're mowing us down! Get everyone out of here!'"

THE DEVIL KING IS OUT OF THE OFFICE (4)

Just as Emeralda was heading off to MgRonald to eat dinner and snoop on Emi and Chiho, a thundering roar from inside Castle Ereniem sent the pigeons roosting in the building's unique steeple flying into the air.

"I swear to you, I hate every man, woman, and child in this country!!" The large man leaped out from his tiny desk, paperwork thrown into the air like sparks from a campfire.

"Enough, Albert. People have been sent to tribunals for less reason than this tirade of yours."

Albert Ende, by far the largest of the Hero's quest companions, was raging like a hungry predator, darting from here and there as he fumed to himself—but the woman with him didn't bat an eye.

"Oh, shut up, Hazel! I hate you, too! I can't take this any longer!!"

This wasn't a battlefield, so she was in civilian clothing, but the dignity she exuded was impossible to hide. It was General Hazel Rumack, chief director of the Federated Order of the Five Continents and the de facto leader of Saint Aile's military branch.

"No wonder Eme never wants to come back! I've never seen a bunch of people as malicious and treacherous as you idiots from the West!"

"And what will telling me that accomplish, Director Ende?"

Rumack's icy rejoinder was met with more hellfire from Albert. "'Director' now, is it? All right, yes! I *am* acting director of the Holy Magic Administrative Institute! But I can't sub in for a real court sorcerer, all right? And yet I have all these pricks at the Institute going on like *ooh, Emeralda would have handled it in the blink of an eye* with one another, right in front of my face so I can hear it! If you don't like me that much, I'll happily resign right this minute! Just get that broccoli-haired li'l girl back for me! It's not like I'm sitting on this ridiculously tiny chair because I think it's comfortable!"

"So idle chatter from the sorcerers is enough to set you off? You are rather more thin-skinned than I thought." Rumack raised a surprised eyebrow. "I'll admit to being biased, but the sorcerers and researchers here live in their own little world, you could say. You wouldn't be so angry if you just accepted that dealing with them will occasionally rankle you."

"Oh, I am well past that point, thank you! Why do *I* have to scrutinize this research report analyzing the density of holy force in the atmosphere?! And that'd be one thing, but why do I need those snot-nosed brats sniffing their noses at me the whole time?! *Oooh, look at this, you messed it up again*—shut up already!"

"You have quite a bit of pent-up rage, I see. By the way, I've come here because one of my students is crying at me about how he's too scared to ask you about the status of his draft report."

"Yeah? You talkin' about the kid from that noble family with the crazy, fancy-pants armor on? I saw him today! If he thinks that shiny armor would ever save his ass in the battlefield, he's got another thing comin', lemme tell you! The enemy would aim their holy magic at him first!"

"Their mission is not to serve as frontline troops. They serve as decoration for the imperial castle. They polish up that armor until you can see your reflection in it. That armor won't face a blade or an arrow once in its life. They are paid to look fancy, to make the emperor's castle shine so brightly that royal guests can see them a mile away."

"Oh, well, isn't that nice?! And I bet they get paid a hell of a lot more than the grunts duking it out in the Central Continent with the demons and the other islands! This entire world's got its priorities screwed up!"

"You will find no disagreement from me on that point, but would you want to spend your life in their armored boots? You would find it powerfully boring in short order."

"Yeah, and they'd probably never even notice how boring their lives are! And if they don't, I sure as hell ain't gonna tell them!"

"Oh, brother…"

Rumack gave the fuming Albert a look, then wadded up the research draft request in her hand and tossed it in the wastebasket next to the desk.

The Holy Magic Administrative Institute, led by the sorcerer Emeralda Etuva, was a government office under direct control of the emperor. On paper, it was an independent entity from the knight corps, and thus requests from the knights had to be submitted in document form. So basically, what had just happened was Rumack formally asking Albert for her student's draft back and Albert refusing.

"Would you like to go for a drink, maybe? I imagine the walls of the city are too constricting for someone from the great expanses of the North like you. Perhaps a walk around the castle town would do you good."

"Sure, if you don't mind me ditching this job for good!"

"That would be rather more troublesome than I prefer. If you run from us, you will be a wanted man across the empire."

Rumack didn't think he would actually go through with it. But for safety's sake, the place she chose for this drink was her own office—an unadorned, almost barren little room, not at all befitting a woman of her stature.

"Wow. Exciting place."

"Sometimes, you see, being a woman can be a weakness in itself. I am not that much of a patriot for my own people."

The only real décor to speak of was a suit of ceremonial armor, each part of it polished and sharpened to a fine edge.

"I've obtained something uncommon for us to drink. In terms of looks, I cannot recommend it to those with more refined tastes, but as someone who has traveled the world as much as you have, I would not hesitate to let you try it."

"Oh?"

Rumack fished a hand into the nether regions of a bookshelf, producing a bottle from it. Albert's eyes burst open.

"Southern Island liquor?"

"I thought you would recognize it."

The large, nondescript bottle of liquor was infused with the full body of a gigantic, grotesque-looking lizard. It was a familiar sight to Albert.

"They say only the aristocracy in the desert lands know how to make this. Have you had it before?"

"I didn't know they made liquor out of those guys. Y'know, once you finish this bottle, you can chop up the lizard inside, sprinkle some spices on it, roast it on skewers over a charcoal fire, and damn, you got yourself a good dinner."

The thin, light-copper liquid poured into Rumack's silver tumblers practically reeked of alcohol. But take a swig, and it had a surprisingly soft touch upon the tongue, as if gently caressing you from the throat to the stomach. It was habit-forming.

"Not bad."

"There, see?" Rumack poured another serving into Albert's tumbler glass. "So, what else did Emeralda tell you?"

"Huh?"

"She couldn't have extended her stay in that other world on a whim."

"Heh. You'd be surprised. I'm sure all she really wants is a couple more nice meals in her belly before she leaves. I guess there's some kinda religious holiday coming up, and it features lots of dishes that're only served around that time."

Albert took a lighter sip this time, sloshing the liquid around a bit on his tongue.

"If that's what she really wants, then what was her excuse for it?"

"Ah..." Albert slumped into the room's sofa, despite not being invited to. "It sounds like Emilia wants to study at a university. One over there, I mean. And Eme wants to help her out."

"Oh!" Rumack's eyes opened wide. The concept sounded fun to her. "So this...Japan, allows common women like her access to higher education?"

Such institutions were open only to nobility—male nobility—in Saint Aile. The Church's religious school, despite claims of being open to the general populace regardless of upbringing, had largely devolved into someplace for the less powerful of young aristocrats to go to. Its student body had a bunch of fancy family names and little else, so if a commoner were to blunder their way into class, they would quickly be ostracized and bullied right back out.

"Your upbringing doesn't matter, apparently. They charge a lot of money, though."

"They do? I suppose we can't fund her from here, then."

Albert looked at the surface of the liquid in his glass. "Ahh, even if there was a money changer, something tells me Emilia wouldn't accept our charity anyway."

"True enough," Rumack replied, smiling a little as the almost-choking scent of alcohol wafted up from her tumbler. "If we can make the Hero Emilia owe us a favor, that could give us an advantage in any possible situation we run into in Ente Isla. Perhaps she intends never to return at all, just for that reason."

"You look happy about that."

"Of course. I don't want her to come back."

Albert knew all too well that Rumack really meant it.

"The events in Heavensky have been reported far more widely than I expected."

These events, of course, meant the news that both Emilia the Hero and Alciel the Great Demon General were still alive.

"Emilia and Alciel," she continued, "are no longer in Ente Isla, but they were both seen by throngs of people. Word of this will grow diluted the farther away it spreads, but regardless, there will always be a sommelier or two who can sniff out what it really is."

"But do you think any of them will realize there's another world involved?"

"The possibility of that is well beyond zero, I would say. Both demons and angels actually exist, after all."

Rumack herself was a devout member of the Church but not enough of a zealot to believe that the force of her god had a hand in everything that occurred in the world.

"If Emilia came back here, you know she'd never be happy. We could perhaps rebuild Sloane and have the knights ensure it remains a secret, but it would be all too easy to have word leak out about it. The mere existence of the name Emilia Justina will forever have to come at the cost of something else."

Emilia the Hero was born in the Saint Aile village of Sloane. Ever since she'd defeated Lucifer's forces and became a savior to humanity, Saint Aile had used her name for their own political, financial, and military advantage. This was fine back when mankind, united by a common foe in the Devil King's Army, had Saint Aile perform most of the heavy lifting in the war. Now, without that common foe, things were different. While the other nations and continents were aware that Emilia was from Saint Aile, it was now Saint Aile struggling to figure out Emilia's treatment and affiliation.

Sloane was considered to be a satellite settlement under the jurisdiction of the walled city of Cassius. The previous prince who ruled over Cassius's domain was part of Pippin Magnus's faction, and after the events in Heavensky caused Pippin's downfall, this prince was also forced to take the heat. But the prince's family hadn't disappeared. Pippin's faction no longer had a public presence, but there were countless numbers of strategic marriages and other alliances designed to keep the prince's line going. Several of the people involved wielded great power in other regions or nations; attempting to force them all out would just invite rancor from other nobles in and around Cassius.

Currently, a prince loyal to Rumack from the family had been appointed to run the region, ensuring that the Cassius name continued and the previous prince's crimes were atoned for. If Emilia decided to return to Sloane and live a quiet life outside the public eye, she'd still be the strongest human being in the world. Her mere presence would give the ruler of Cassius overwhelming amounts of power. And while people using her good name were one thing, some of the rank-and-file nobles would no doubt attempt to use her dignity as a woman to gain clout with the ruling prince, as well as Rumack and the Saint Aile emperor.

In short, there were no doubt at least a few greedy nobles in Cassius who wanted to marry Emilia to boost their own name. And there was no way Emilia's disposition would allow that.

"I suppose she'll have to remain single her whole life, hmm? Like me."

"Oh? I heard a rumor that the crown prince himself is after the Hazel Rumack name."

"Hmm. Well. I am not going to sit here and say 'I don't want a man who doesn't want me for myself' like a little girl, but I doubt I could ever love some would-be big shot whose greatest talent is polishing his armor."

"Ha! That'd earn you more than just a tribunal. Insulting the imperial court could merit the death penalty."

Albert loved how Rumack never minced words.

"If Emilia ever fell in love with a commoner, I'm sure he would be dead under mysterious circumstances before long. Marrying into the aristocracy would plunge her straight into political strife. Someone with a nice suit of armor wouldn't be near enough for her."

"Heroes only truly exist in legend after all, I s'pose."

"You said it," Rumack replied as she corked the bottle of lizard wine and hid it in a corner of the shelf. "The only other way is if she was born into a world that didn't know what Heroes were at all. If there's anything I can do for her right now, I suppose it'd just be to ensure she doesn't regret saving Ente Isla."

"You think she's that narrow-minded?"

"When you grow up, you know, you start noticing things you didn't as a child."

Rumack may have looked young, but she was actually old enough that her current government position wasn't unusual at all for her age. She was closer to Albert in years than Emeralda. That was why, even more than Emeralda, she felt incredibly obliged to this woman over a decade younger than her, forced to carry the entire world on her shoulders. Her work responsibility, and the distance kept between her and Emilia, prevented her from expressing it very often.

"If I could find a way to create a world Emilia could be happy in," she continued, "I gladly would. But I doubt that's what she wants from me. I imagine she thinks of me as just another uniformed officer, ready to take advantage of her good name whenever the opportunity presents itself."

Albert gave an ill-intentioned grin as Rumack glumly averted her eyes. "Oh, I wouldn't worry about that. Emilia has people over there who don't care about her obligations here. They're willing to listen to Emilia gripe on end about them."

"Hmph... And who are you referring to?"

"Mm?"

Albert looked down at Rumack's curious eyes. He sighed, realizing what she wanted him to say.

"Well, the girl Chiho Sasaki and the young woman Rika Suzuki to name two. They are both coworkers of Emilia's. Crestia Bell, too, has proven a reliable friend. She belongs to the Church, but she's never pushy about it, which she likes."

"Haaah..." Rumack visibly winced at Albert's reply, no longer hiding her dissatisfaction. "This is so silly! What's with all that stuff?"

"What do you mean?"

"This is exactly why people are bad-mouthing you up and down the Institute! If I'm here feeding you liquor, the least you could do is entertain me!"

How unfair could you get?

"Pfft. You guys are just gonna pick on me either way. Me, I just gotta work things out so it's as little extra stress on me as possible."

"Ha! Emeralda's taught you too well, I see. You pick up on things so quickly, it's honestly boring."

"Whether I do or not, I'd figure that makes me more approachable than some whiny lady."

"I suppose we'll both have to be happy staying single our whole lives."

"The nomads of the North ain't into settling down. Thanks for the fancy booze. I'll put that draft you mentioned on the top of my to-do pile."

Leaving Rumack to stew in her own juices, Albert marched right back to the Holy Magic Administrative Institute. As he did, he looked through the windows that dotted the hallways, staring at the people in the holy city below. It made him reflect on how people could lead such simple lives, and yet the world they lived in was so incredibly complicated.

"...Ugh. Look at me. That fancy stuff didn't get me *that* drunk."

Saint Aile shouldn't have been particularly tough for Emilia to live in. There were many places outside of Sloane where she could live in relatively secure hiding, and if she went and made a name for herself in Japan, then she'd be shackled to that place in her own way.

"Compared to that, I suppose the Devil King's got it pretty easy, huh?"

Albert had faced off against many demons in his life, not least of which was Adramelech, leader of the enemy forces in the Northern Island. He knew demons weren't a pack of brainless animals. They had their own society, and their king no doubt had his own issues to deal with—but when it came to life in Japan, the Hero Emilia and Satan the Devil King took off from two different starting lines.

Satan had appeared in Ente Isla as king, and he fled to Japan as a king. Emilia became the Hero through no desire of her own, and when she attempted to live up to the responsibility that brought, she was cast adrift before washing up in Japan. Satan never fulfilled his dream of conquering the world, but he was still walking down a path he chose for himself. Emilia saw world peace in her own time, but it was nothing she had ever volunteered for.

Albert didn't know if Emeralda picked up on that difference, but given how fervently she wanted to support Emilia's dreams, she must have understood that incontrovertible fact. One often heard tales of people who went down roads they never expected to take, only to find a different sort of ideal for themselves at the end—and that was likely the only way Emilia would ever find happiness now. Just as Rumack estimated, there was no place left for Emilia in Ente Isla. The mere existence of her name was forever going to hurt someone.

"So she should just play at being the Hero and bicker with the Devil King in Japan forever?"

Something about that didn't sit well with him. The world owed Emilia a tremendous debt. The least it could do was repay the favor a little bit. Where did this world get off, so hell-bent on trying to milk her for everything she had?

"Not that I want the world to fall apart or nothin', but…"

The world just had to learn not to rely on Emilia too much. With both her and the Devil King now in Japan, it had proven more than capable of that.

"A bit like a kid left at home alone who wants his parents to spoil him when they get back, eh…?"

While the Hero and Devil King were away, Ente Isla had somehow managed to keep itself going. But if the guardian they relied on were to return, it'd be just like that child, succumbing to its own greedy desires. If the Devil King were to join her, the world truly would be beyond help—and unfortunately for everyone on it, the god they'd turn to for help was starting to look pretty doubtful herself.

Just as the news of Emilia and Alciel's return had spread world-wide, word was starting to leak out about the betrayal of Olba

Meiyer, one of the six archbishops who led the Church. Church leaders, ex-Pippin loyalists, the Eastern Island politicians who allowed Olba to guide the demons in their directions—potential sources for these leaks lay everywhere.

"Peace is harder than it sounds, huh? It's a lot simpler to keep fightin'."

Albert griped to himself all the way back to the bleak, depressing Holy Magic Administrative Institute. He fished out the wadded-up draft request from the waste bin.

"Hmm... A draft request to send researchers out to investigate holy force densities around holy areas... Oh, right, I heard about this. Umm, I think it talks about the Church around here..."

Albert leafed through his pile of papers—all business he had been forced to delay over the past few days—until he found the draft he was looking for.

"Here we go. I had put this off 'til later because they were asking for thirty researchers or some such nonsense. What're they, crazy? We're already short on people. Why'd they throw a proposal with the Church's fingerprints all over it to us, of all people?"

It appeared to be a proposal to investigate the source of the holy water taken from Sankt Ignoreido, the holy land and headquarters of the Church. This water was used for ceremonies, the holy power infused within making it useful for treatment in Church hospitals, but the quality of this liquid had fallen as of late. Relations between the Church and Emeralda's Institute had deteriorated since the show trial she was subjected to, but Saint Aile was still in close contact with them, so the relationship hadn't been cut off entirely. A lot of Institute researchers still bore a grudge against the Church, however, so Albert taking up a Church job while Emeralda was gone would no doubt hurt his reputation among them even further.

"Ugggghhhh... Get your ass back here, Eme..."

A decline in holy water quality directly affected people's lives. It could even affect the dignity of the Church itself. The Institute (and by extension, Saint Aile) solving a problem that the Church's own scholars couldn't handle would earn them some useful brownie points, which is why this issue was now on Albert's desk.

"A striking decline in the water's holy force content, though…? Maybe there was a cave-in somewhere and the underground streams changed direction or something?"

Albert raised an eyebrow as he affixed the Institute's formal seal of approval on the request and began listing the people he'd ask to join the project.

◊

"Caiel and Sikeena's objective was to eradicate the immortality tech. They went around the place, destroying any data and equipment we had related to that project. No way any regular security force coulda handled them, right? It wound up being me, Satanael, and Camael as the last line of defense against 'em. It was an insane battle! If we didn't have Satanael around, with his understanding of their DNA structure, that probably woulda been the end for me."

Gabriel visibly shivered. For the first time, Chiho sensed that this angel, who breezily fought off the Hero and Devil King at the same time, could feel genuine fear after all.

"But didn't Caiel and Sikeena help Ignora with that research? Why would they do that?"

It was an obvious question, one that Gabriel had anticipated in advance.

"They didn't think Ignora was as talented as she turned out to be. They didn't expect lending her a hand would lead to this crazy discovery. Maybe they figured she'd stumble upon a more direct solution to the pandemic, a vaccine or something, long before then. But to the Sephirah children, making immortality into a real-life thing kinda put the whole human race in danger."

The Sephirah interfered with the course of human history only when mankind faced a danger it couldn't handle by itself. The lack of progress fending off the pandemic definitely counted as that. But the Sephirah's involvement inadvertently led to humanity discovering immortality—in a way, an even graver threat.

"Like, think about it, 'kay? If we all woke up tomorrow and people just stopped dying, what'd happen to the world?"

A population explosion. Worldwide famines. Territorial wars. All that and more flashed across the minds of everyone at the table. That wasn't what Caiel and Sikeena lent a hand to Ignora for—and that was why they raided the lab: to eliminate this mortal danger from the universe.

"But you know what happened? Satanael and Camael did it. After this long protracted battle, they actually beat them. Maybe it was because they both had a grip on Caiel's and Sikeena's DNA. I dunno. But that's how it turned out, and that's when Ente Isla's troubles began."

The lunar laboratory had fended off the threat from the Sephirah children. But now it was facing a completely different threat from its home planet. All the nations down there had independently reached the same conclusion—this attack on the lab was being carried out by one country or another, in hopes of locking up the research results for themselves.

Soon, it resulted in war—one that ultimately never ended. Every nation deployed troops to the lab, under the pretext of keeping their own researchers secure. On the ground, in the air, in space, and on the lunar surface, they all set about killing one another. The researchers and colonists, faced with a sight they never expected to see when they finally reached their research goals, decided that drastic measures had to be taken. Those measures: full-scale evacuation.

If the lab was going to be broken into little pieces by these nations, the immortality tech would be lost forever. The home planet had gone well and truly insane; the lab could try pleading with the nations all it wanted, but at this rate, its research was as good as lost already.

Thus, Ignora and her team waved good-bye. Gabriel joined them as head of security, along with a portion of the colonists. All the colony cities were set up to be operable as mobile space bases in case of emergency—a measure set up by treaties in the early stages of space development, so that no single country could seize them all. In the end, this measure allowed the colonies to flee from their home planet forever.

All the world's armies could do was look on resentfully as the colonies took off from the moon. Attacking them might cause them to lose the immortality tech forever; anyone who tried it would face the wrath of the entire rest of the world.

"But even at that point," Laila said with a sad shake of the head, "the nations of our world couldn't stop fighting. They told us not to run, to side with this or that nation. They never truly understood what we were running from."

Filled with despair for her native planet, Ignora set a course for the colonies beyond the event horizon.

"And just as the planet and its moon had disappeared from view, our holy force scanner picked up an unexpected reaction. Our ultra-long-range optical telescope picked up that old, withered tree—slowly separating itself from the moon."

"Mankind has ended."

"I am sorry, Da'at."

Nobody was around to hear those words exchanged by Caiel and Sikeena, captured after their bloody battle, before they disappeared into thin air.

It was only later when Ignora and the rest of the lunar colonists and researchers found out via their long-range scanners that all the other colonies, as well as the main cities of their home planet, had vanished. This they found out a mere ten years later, as they were floating around the outskirts of their star system. Just like that, they had lost any connection to the universe—and all that remained was a long, so unimaginably long era of wandering across space.

"So," said Laila, "as I think you can see now, our wandering ended when we came across the moon of Ente Isla. Our holy force scanners picked up the same waveforms from it that we saw with the tree on the dark side of our own moon."

"And that...!!"

Emi gasped. Laila gravely nodded at her.

"And right next to that moon, we saw a world exactly like our own. So we chose it as our second homeland. But at the time...Ente Isla still had only one moon."

THE TEEN AND THE CALL-CENTER LADY RING IN THE NEW YEAR CONT'D

"Why...? Why did it have to turn out like this?!"

Rika's shouts, after Chiho finally told her the whole story, echoed their despondent way across the empty shell of Room 201.

"We were all gonna spend Christmas here for Alas Ramus! We weren't gonna worry about all of the baggage from Emi's mom's! We'd forget about fighting, we'd leave the people in heaven and Ente Isla to deal with their own crap, and we'd worry about our own lives for a change! What happened to all of that?!"

"The Christmas party," Chiho replied, not a shred of emotion on her face, "never happened."

"Huh...?"

"Emeralda went home first. Then Suzuno. Yusa and Alas Ramus were next, along with Nord and Laila. Maou, Ashiya, Urushihara, and Acieth went last. That was on the twenty-sixth."

"The twenty-sixth? You were talking about holding the party then..."

"We were counting more on the twenty-third, actually, since it's a national holiday."

The birthday of Japan's currently reigning emperor was always treated as a national holiday. In the case of Emperor Akihito, that date is December twenty-third.

"We decided to go with that since it'd be easier for you to join us, Rika. But they all decided to go back to Ente Isla before the twenty-third rolled around, and…three days later…"

"They left you behind?"

"…Yeah."

"But that… That's terrible! I thought you were all supposed to be friends! And you didn't even hold the party you were all planning?!"

"I couldn't do anything about it. About anything. One statement was all it took to turn it all on its head. Something so strong it even made Urushihara resolve to fight it out."

"But… But they all had their own motivations, their own things they wanted to do. So why…?"

The stone-faced Chiho cracked a light smile. "We couldn't win. None of us could. Not when *that's* what we were told."

"Chiho…"

What could've transpired to make Chiho—a girl far stronger than Rika, someone who had dealt with these visitors for so much longer than her—concede so easily like this? Rika couldn't even begin to guess what had happened.

"Laila was pretty surprised about it. You know, Maou and Yusa had been so stubborn with her for so long, and then they both just said yes. She kept asking them if they were sure about it—her and Gabriel. And not just those two. She asked me; she asked Ashiya, Urushihara, Suzuno, Emeralda, Nord; she wanted to be sure we were all on board for it. And we said yes. *I* said yes. I had to. I wasn't forced to. That was just the only thing I could've said to her."

The fact that Chiho offered no resistance whatsoever was a shock to Rika.

"It was that convincing?"

"And I couldn't choose to fight with them, either. I don't have that kind of power."

Chiho sighed slightly, her breath given a white sheen by the cold of the room.

"I apologize that it took this long to tell you, Rika."

"…It's all right. I had the worst trouble facing up to Emi and Ashiya anyway, and I had some family stuff pop up back at home, so I was stuck over there for a while…but… But wow, they're gone, huh? I sent Emi a New Year's card, you know."

Emi mentioned that she missed her chance to send any New Year's greetings last year, so Rika went through the trouble of making a handwritten card and sending it to Emi's place from Kobe. That card was now undoubtedly shivering inside her mailbox at Urban Heights Eifukucho.

"So…when'll we see them again? This isn't, like, *it*, is it?"

"…Um."

"They're off to defeat this god…um, Ignora, right? That's gonna take a really long time, isn't it? But it's not like it'll be just constant fighting day after day, don't you think? They have to be able to make it back here sometime."

"I don't know. I didn't know then, either—like, what's waiting for them over there, so…"

Chiho unsteadily rose up. Rika was still sprawled out on the floor, unable to stand. She couldn't accept this—but it really had been the reality all along. There were these people who never should've been here, and now they were back where they belonged, on their own free will. Neither Rika nor Chiho had any right to stop them.

There was no man named Sadao Maou in this world. There was no woman named Emi Yusa, either. Everyone was back in the world where they belonged, in the form they should've been in all along.

"So…"

The world where they belonged.

"So I really can't accept that. We can't wait that long, can we?"

Rika, her heart ruled by a great emptiness now that the world was back to what it *should* have been, looked up at Chiho.

"I don't know how long it'll take," she spat out, her voice dry and scratchy. "I don't know if they'll ever come back alive. We can't wait for a battle like that to end."

She undid the scarf covering the bottom of her head and tossed it on the floor.

"Ch-Chiho?"

And that wasn't all. She removed the bag she had on her back, threw her coat down on the ground, then ran over to the front door and put on her shoes, running back with Rika's shoes as well.

"Chiho? What're you doing?!"

"Rika! Put these on! Right here!"

"H-here? What, on the tatami mats? Hey, Chiho, get ahold of yourself..."

"This is something I just can't put up with. I can't wait that long. I couldn't wait that long. Could you, Rika?!"

"Wh-whaaa?!"

Now Rika was being jostled around by the collar, Chiho almost pulling her up off the floor.

"Maou never answered me! I told him months and months ago that I loved him! I said just a bit ago to give me the answer if he thinks he has one! And then he forgot all about it and let that single statement drive him to go! How long am I supposed to even wait?! Don't you think he could've at least given me a timeline?! Despite all this love I have for him?!"

"Huh? Huh? Wha—?!"

"You have to agree with me, don't you, Rika?! You never got an answer from Ashiya, either! Is this how you want everything to end? That can't be good for you, can it?! You want an answer, right?!"

"Uh? A-an answer? You mean about my love? But I already, uh—"

"Did Ashiya say that he *didn't* like you, Rika?!"

"Uhh? Whaaat?"

"Did he say *I love you*, or *I hate you*, or *Let's be a couple*, or *I can't be with you*, or *Let's just be friends*, or *I don't wanna see you again*?! He didn't, did he?! You were crying, weren't you, Rika?! If he made you cry, the *least* he could've said was something like *Don't come back here again* or whatever! They're always like this! And maybe they see it as a way of being nice, but they've kept it up for so long, it's not convincing anyone anymore! Is it?! Ashiya went off without even telling you what his feelings were, didn't he?! Doesn't that annoy you at all?!"

"I, um, uhh…"

"If he can't stand to be around you, why can't he just say that?! Instead he just phrases it to try and make *you* give up instead! That's so unfair! And after all this time, Maou's still like *I don't know, I don't know*! Then what does he know?!"

"C-calm down, Chiho! What's going on with you?! Why are you…?"

"Look, I'm past being the nice little Chi who sits on her bed, hands on knees, waiting for everyone important to her to get back here! I'm past it! That's what I've decided! So!"

She released Rika, then reached down toward the edge of one of the tatami mats lining the floor.

"Hnnnnngh!"

"Ch-Chiho?! What're you doing?!"

"I'm ripping this tatami mat off! Help me out!"

"O-okay?!"

Rika lent a hand to Chiho, not a single clue what it was all leading to. The mat came up easily…and revealed nothing but bare floorboards. It wasn't hiding anything—she still had no idea what Chiho was doing. But something was odd about these floors. It was almost too clean. The bottom sides of tatami mats like this one usually grew dusty over time, the baseboards getting stained and cracking here or there. Meanwhile, the floor here almost looked freshly polished.

"We can't fight," a determined Chiho declared. "We can't fly, we can't swing a sword, and we can't breathe fire. If we fall off a building, we die. If the expressway overpass falls down, I can't fix it. But…I know how to cook!"

"Huh?"

"I know what Maou likes to eat! Him, and Yusa, and Ashiya, and Urushihara, and Suzuno, and Alas Ramus, too! I know what they don't like! I know how to clean! I'm learning how to sew! If someone has a problem, I can listen to them whine for a while! If I have my phone with me, I can cast an Idea Link! And I can swear up and down that I was a close friend of everyone who ever set foot here in Room 201! So!"

Then Chiho took something out of her pocket. It was small and light in her hand, emitting a faint glow, and she lifted it high into the air and smashed it against the bare floor.

"Agh!!"

Rika instinctively covered her face. The floorboards suddenly lit up, the surface shimmering like an oily film. The light grew stronger and stronger, forcing Rika to shut her eyes.

"What—what is that, Chiho?!"

"Wait just a minute. The border surface will stabilize enough in a moment to connect to the other side."

"Connect to… Ahh?!"

A final, intense flash of light coursed across the room, then subsided.

"You can open your eyes now."

"Wh-what on…?"

At Chiho's signal, Rika put her hand down. For a few moments, she stared, astonished, at where the floorboards used to be. Now it was a spring of light, pulsing shades of white and blue. The remaining five tatami mats in the room, cracked and sun bleached, were now home to an almost divine well of eerie light. It was so beyond the realm of common sense, Rika couldn't even begin to explain it.

"I think you've seen this at least once before, Rika. In Ueno."

"Ueno… Ah!!" Rika gasped, realizing what this meant. "Suzuno, in front of the *Gates of Hell* sculpture… So this is…"

"Right." Chiho nodded, her voice a little shaky. "This is a Gate. A magical tunnel connecting one world to another across the stars."

It was the same path to another world that Maou and Suzuno opened over in Ueno Park, on their way to saving Emi and Ashiya.

"Here we go."

"Huh?"

Before she knew it, Rika found her hand being taken. Somewhere along the line, Chiho had picked up the bag she had dropped on the floor, along with Rika's satchel. Her eyes were pointed right on the light beneath her.

"W-wait! Go where?"

"You don't get carsick or anything, do you, Rika? It was pretty rough on me the first time, so I brought some antinausea pills with me. If you think you need them along the way, go ahead and take them, okay?"

"Along the way? I... What? What are you talking about, Chiho? Like, really, where are we..."

"Here we go!"

"Where are we *goooooooooooooooooooooooooooooooiiing*?!"

An unexpectedly strong force was dragging Rika, hand in hand with Chiho, right into the spring of light. The floor that was there turned into an empty space, no foothold in sight. Rika was struck with fear as she plunged into what felt like thin air.

The falling seemed to go on forever until, just for a single moment, she felt something lightly patting her tensed shoulders. Considering they were falling, it didn't really seem like there was anything to land on. There wasn't any wind or anything else to indicate how fast the fall was. Gingerly, she opened her eyes, only to find something she had seen in movies and photos before, but that almost nobody would ever get a chance to truly see in person.

"No way."

It was Earth, a giant blue planet before her eyes—and now that Rika discovered she was floating in space, she realized it was rapidly shrinking. The Earth, the moon, the light of the sun all faded, giving way to an undulating tunnel of pure light around her.

"Over here. Follow me."

"Ch-Chiho!"

Chiho had touched her from behind, both bags still on her. Beckoning to Rika, she started traveling down the tunnel of light.

From Rika's vantage point, it almost looked like she was flying. She wasn't moving her arms or legs at all; instead, she simply focused on the direction she needed to go. Realizing she was going farther and farther away, Rika tried her best to catch up—and just thinking of it gave her the sensation that she was going forward herself.

She wondered if it was a dream, if everything she saw here was a figment of her imagination and she'd be back in the Sasazuka she knew, with Emi and Ashiya.

"If anything happens, use this, okay?"

But the feel of the barf bag and bottle of liquid antinausea medication Chiho gave her, as they flew side by side with each other, seemed too real to be a dream. There was certainly nothing dreamy about them anyway.

"Chiho! What—what's all this…?!"

Rika finally managed to get the question out. Chiho's reply failed to clear up much of anything.

"We're inside the Gate. Right now, we're flying down the path the Gate opened for us."

"F-flying?!"

"It's gonna take a little time. I got kind of sick my first time, so let me know if that happens to you."

"Time? Huh? What was all that just now?! This is a Gate? Like, through space?!"

"It's a spell that connects between worlds. We just jumped out of Earth, on our way to our destination."

"Our… Where?!"

"Where do you think?"

Chiho's cheerful smile seemed downright terrifying to Rika right now.

"The world our lovers are on."

Rika woke up to a scent she was familiar with—the smell of tatami mats.

"Huh…? I…"

Slowly, her eyes opened, rewarding her with the sight of a tatami-mat floor.

"…It was a dream?"

It was a pretty crazy one—her and Chiho, flying through space. There was this secret door to another world under the tatami-mat floor of Room 201 at Villa Rosa Sasazuka, and they jumped right through it and outside of Earth.

"Nnnnh… Huh?"

Then Rika noticed the unnatural amount she was sweating. It was really hot inside this room.

"Wait… Did Maou's room have a heater…?"

Her eyes gradually came into focus.

"………?!"

Then she could feel the blood drain from her head. She was right—she *was* on a tatami-mat floor. But this wasn't the one in Room 201.

"Uh… Whaaaaaa?!"

If Rika was familiar with the term *redoubt*, she would have used it here. It was a hard floor she found herself on, one that seemed to go on forever in all directions. Looking up, she found a ceiling that seemed cloaked in darkness. Large pillars, like the trunks of some primeval forest, were lined up in neat rows, and next to her, an altar the size of a small mountain.

It was a vast, unnerving space, one whose stone, or brick, or earthen surfaces seemed to echo Rika's screams forever, and in some areas, it seemed oddly dilapidated. Looking closely at the floor, she could spot holes all over the place, and some of the columns were falling apart. It could only be described as an ancient temple or ruin of some sort, and she had no idea at all why she woke up atop a floor of six tatami mats neatly arranged in the middle of it.

"Huh? Is this…?"

Still recovering from the shock, Rika looked around her surroundings, only to find something else lying on the mats.

"Oh, this is Maou's…"

It was something she was as familiar with as the mats themselves—a cheap *kotatsu* table that had been used and abused for far too long.

Then, in this space that barely seemed real, someone else's voice rang out.

"What...? What is this for...?"

"Ah?!"

The room was too large to make it clear where the voice came from. Her head swiveled around again. Then she heard it—a rhythmic thudding, as if a couple of heavy objects were being struck against each other. The sound soon took on a more familiar shape.

"Oh, good, Rika, you're awake."

"Emi...?"

It was Emi Yusa, Rika's best friend. She was dressed in some kind of ethnic clothing unfamiliar to Rika, but her face, her hair, her eyes, and her voice were unmistakable.

"Emi, where are we...?"

"I'm sorry I didn't say anything!"

"Agh?!"

Without answering the question, Emi hugged Rika, her voice ringing out almost in alarm.

"I was in such a rush, there wasn't time to talk. I thought about going back to talk things over with you, but then all this stuff piled up over here, so I kept getting delayed... I guess it's the New Year now, huh? I'm so sorry!"

"Ahh... Yeah, uh, um..."

Rika noticed the smell of Emi's preferred brand of shampoo on her, along with other pointless things, as her slow voice plodded along.

"Um, where are we? What are the tatami mats from Maou's place doing in this weird chamber?"

"...Oh, right. Wow, Rika, you don't know anything yet!" Emi hurriedly undid herself from their embrace and clapped her hands. "But aren't you hot? Take off your coat first. It's winter here, too, but we're so close to the equator that it's always pretty warm."

"Huh? Um, okay."

Rika followed her instructions. Freeing herself of the cocoon of heat inside the coat made it quickly feel cooler.

"Can you stand up? Oh, put these on. These floors are pretty cold."

Emi pointed to a pair of what looked like leather slippers next to the mats.

"Um, Emi? I think I jumped in through the floor at Maou's place."

"Yeah, Chiho told me. She pretty much forced you along without explaining anything, huh?"

"Uh, yeah. Like, I'm really not dreaming, am I?"

"Who knows? It's like a dream to me."

Emi did appear to be in high spirits, grabbing Rika's hand as they navigated the gigantic space.

"I always wanted to show you my homeland, after all."

"Your...homeland?"

After a while, they finally reached the edge of the space. There was a window here, looking like it was gouged into the wall, and Rika sleepily surmised that the blue on the other side was the sky.

"Some people might get angry at me for saying it...but I think the view from here is probably the best."

"Oh..."

Following Emi's lead, Rika put her hand on the window frame and looked outside.

"Rika, welcome to Ente Isla, Land of the Holy Cross."

The window, it turned out, was pretty high up. The perfectly flat blue sky extended all the way to the horizon, the prairie way down below spreading out far and wide into forests, roads, marshes, and lakes as far as the eye could see. A flock of birds of prey flitted across the air, a species like none Rika recognized from Japan.

"...Ah," she said as she took it all in. It was just so expansive, like

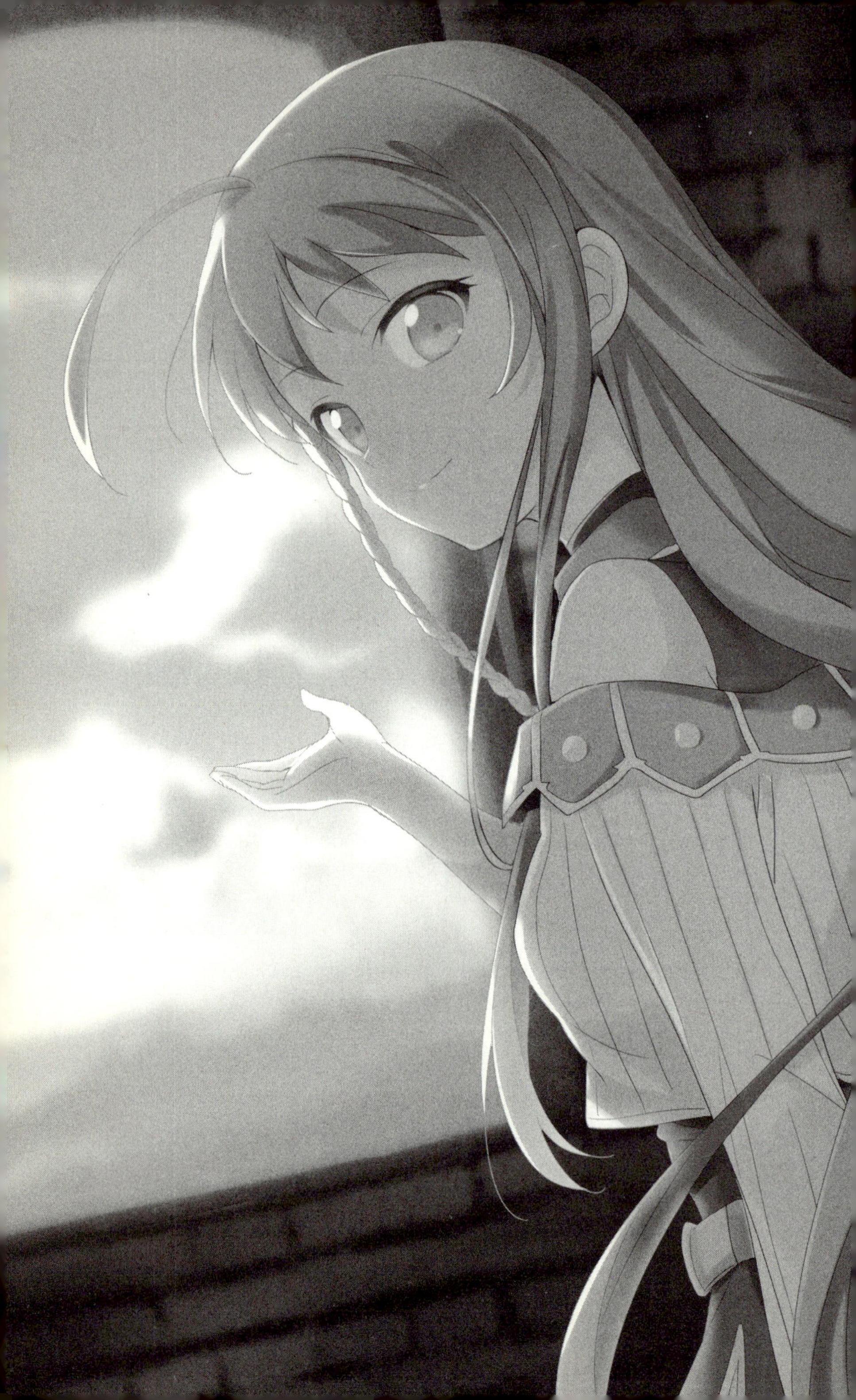

nothing she could see from Kobe Port Tower or Kyoto Tower, and she could tell that people were teeming down below. She could see that, and while she wasn't sure if it was her eyes playing tricks on her from this high up, she felt like she saw some other creatures, things that definitely *seemed* alive but moved and acted like nothing she could even imagine.

"Um......Emi, what did you just say?"

"Hmm?"

"Where are we again?"

"Ente Isla."

"Huh?"

"You're in the main city on Ente Isla's Central Continent. The ruins of what used to be called Isla Centurum."

"Huh? Um, huh?"

"Kinda hard to swallow?" Emi asked, curious about Rika's muted reaction.

Rika nodded deeply, like a puppet whose strings had been cut.

"Well, wanna go down to the surface? It would take a whole day to walk down there, so apologies in advance, but we'll take the quick way."

"Huh? From here? Where to?"

"To the ground level. I bet this'll feel a lot more real to you once you say hello to everyone down there. Pardon me one sec."

"Ah... Ah!"

The next moment, Rika was scooped up in Emi's wispy arms. They both had identical body types, but the sight of Emi picking up a grown woman like she was made of papier-mâché reminded her all over again that this girl wasn't from Earth at all.

But that wasn't the problem. The last time Rika found herself carried like this, it led to assorted terrifying events right afterward, didn't it?

"I won't drop you, but hang on tight for me, okay?"

"Huh? Wait... Emi?"

"Here we go."

Rika in her hands, Emi planted a foot on the window frame they looked out from just a moment ago.

"No, wait a.."

Her voice was lost in the air. She couldn't even scream any longer. Out of nowhere, Rika was flying through a sky she had never seen before.

In front of her wide-open eyes, the ground began to loom closer. But they weren't going fast enough to be in free fall. And when she realized Emi was actually floating down, a lot more slowly than some of the more extreme roller coasters you see in amusement parks, Rika spotted them all—the masses of people on the ground.

"Wha...?"

It was a huge crowd, all dressed in assorted types of clothing and armor. She could spot multiple ethnicities among them. From Rika's perspective, many of them were clearly human. Everyone else, though? Completely different.

"Wha—wha—wha—wha...?"

There were beasts walking on two legs. There were giants literally the size of a house. It wasn't birds flying through the air—it was people shaped like birds. Some of the crowd didn't make it up to the height of a human being's waist. There were walking skeletons, straight from the campfire horror stories of Rika's childhood.

And there, in the middle of this massive throng, was a girl wearing a bandanna and an apron, standing atop a stepladder and using a large mixer to stir the cauldron in front of her. It was Chiho.

"This is Devil's Castle. The *real* one Maou and the other demon officers used to storm Ente Isla."

"Are you kidding meeeeeeeeeeeee?!"

The scream made Emi wince, as much as she seemed to revel in the reaction.

Several of the people (creatures?) in the crowd picked up on Rika's shouting, Chiho among them.

"Ooh! Rika!"

She bounded off the stepladder and ran up to their landing point.

"Wha—wha—whawhawha—!"

"Rika! You're awake! Listen, I'm really sorry! I forgot to explain to you how to land!"

"Seriously, Chiho…" Emi lectured. "I know you were in a hurry, but try to be more careful from now on, okay? If Bell didn't happen to be free just then, we would've had to delay treatment for a while."

"All right! I apologize!" Chiho meekly bowed her head.

"Whawhawhawhawhawha—?"

"Rika? Are you good? Can I put you down now?"

Emi did just that, but it didn't help Rika recognize the sights and sounds around her any. She only managed two or three steps forward before falling to her knees.

"Rika! Are you okay?!"

"Does it still hurt?!"

"The reality," she woozily replied.

"Rika?"

"The reality of it hurts. I mean, you told me all about this, but *this* is a whole different thing. Forgive me if it's kind of freaking me out. Ahh, Ente Isla. This is really it, huh? Ahh…"

Her eyes focused far away.

"Yeah, you sure got me."

"Lady Rika Suzuki, I understand that you have provided both public and private support to the Hero Emilia during her journey in the alien world of Japan. My name is General Hazel Rumack, leader of the Federated Order of the Five Continents. It is a pleasure to meet you."

"S-sure…"

"I am sure some of our customs might seem strange from your perspective, but a friend to the Hero Emilia is a friend to all Ente Isla. If you lack for anything during your stay here, do not hesitate to bring it up with any of us in the Order. We will make sure your needs are promptly attended to."

"S-sure..."

Chiho was followed soon after by another of the Hero Emilia's friends. Rika was quickly hustled over to a rather ornate tent—that belonging to Hazel Rumack, commander of the human forces in the area. To Rika, however, the sight of this clearly executive-looking woman in impossibly ornate-looking armor bowing her head and speaking fluent, polite Japanese to her as she sat upon a fluffy, expensive-looking chair and served tea in a cup so intricately decorated that Rika was afraid to even touch it was a tad difficult to comprehend.

"Hmph. So it's you, eh? The friend of Great Demon General Chiho, the 'MgRonald Barista'?"

Only slightly less difficult to grasp was the creature that now entered the tent behind Chiho, looking a bit like a gigantic praying mantis.

"I am Farfarello! General of the Devil King's Army! And I have come to prepare for the upcoming battle alongside the humans!"

"S-s-sure..."

The demon, whose name would require several repetitions before Rika could get it down, took a glance at Chiho. "Any friend to Her Excellency Chiho is a friend of mine. We demons may not have the consideration for their fellow man the way a human might, but please make yourself at home."

"Th-thanks..."

She couldn't help but notice that one swipe of his serrated forearm could probably lop off both her and Rika's heads, but the demon with the tricky name seemed to be treating Chiho like someone in a higher class than himself.

"Um, Chiho, sorry to bother you..."

"Hmm?"

"Why did he call you a MgRonald Barista?"

Chiho glanced at Rika, then Farfarello. "Um, it's kind of my nickname in the demon realms."

"Uhh..."

No explanation would do much to quell the maelstrom inside Rika's mind right now.

"Chiho, did he just call you 'Her Excellency'? Are you *sure* you're not secretly a fancy wizard or something?"

Rika, face tensed up, looked at Chiho and Emi.

"I mean, where do I even begin with this?"

She looked around the camp. Even after Farfarello left, countless humans and demons were walking to and fro through it on their business. She brought a hand to her stomach.

"Wait. So that guy with the name that sounds like a fabric softener brand—that's a demon?"

"Oh, you mean Farlo?"

"I thought it was longer than that?"

"That's his nickname. Farfarello's too long, so…"

"You give nicknames to demons. Great. But if he's a demon, why am I all right?"

As she now realized, she was feeling none of the pain the full brunt of the Great Demon General Alciel had brought upon her. And considering all the demons milling about, there had to be a ton of dark force in the air.

"I guess you could call it a lucky break," Chiho offered apologetically. "The moment we left the Gate, I forgot to tell you how to land and you kind of hit your head and got knocked out. Suzuno volunteered to treat you, and she cast some holy defense on you so you'd be okay around demonic force to some extent."

Suzuno was, to say the least, livid at Chiho, but that was another story.

"Like, a barrier or something?"

"No, it's activated the holy force in your body to resist demonic energy. Ente Isla is full of holy energy, so it's a lot easier to apply it than in Japan."

"…Ugh, this is making no sense at all to me. It's like you're trying to describe a game to me on a system I don't even own."

"Well, regardless, as long as someone as strong as Maou doesn't go full demon in front of you, you'll be fine around—"

"Oh! Right! Maou!"

The moment she heard the name, Rika shot to her feet, almost knocking that expensive-looking teacup off the side table. She had to lunge at it to avoid disaster.

"Where's Maou?! What's going on?! Tell me what's going on! None of this is making too much sense yet, but I need to know what's up! I know we're on Ente Isla, but why are you acting so naturally around here, Chiho? Tell me! What's up with all the dudes from that apartment in Sasazuka?"

"Um..."

"Where should we start...?"

"Hey, I heard Rika Suzuki was here?"

Chiho and Emi were just giving each other an awkward glance when a face popped up at the tent entrance—a human-looking man who Rika knew well. It was one of the three demons that once, not too long ago, wrecked Emi's world.

"Maou..."

"Hey."

Sadao Maou was dressed in the same jeans and UniClo shirt Rika remembered him in—the kind of thing you'd see on almost any young adult in Japan.

"Oh, uh, happy New Year, Chi."

"Happy New Year to you, too, Maou. I purchased some of the simmered kelp Ashiya asked for, so I'll serve it at the next meal, okay?"

"Emi...is this reality?"

It didn't seem that way to Rika, but the incredibly humdrum conversation Chiho was having with Maou in this fantasy landscape made it all seem like nothing but a dream.

"It sure is," her best friend told her with a content smile. "I'm not sure I really believe it, either, but this is exactly the reality I'm looking for."

*

"It's all Emeralda's fault, y'know, for suggesting that stupid Christmas party in the first place."

Sadao Maou was seated at the *kotatsu* sitting on top of the tatami-mat floor laid out in the throne room, enjoying the kombu kelp Chiho bought for him. It was a scene straight out of Room 201 in Sasazuka.

"She framed the whole thing as something for Alas Ramus's sake, and—you know—if that's how it is, then whether it's at Emi's place or not, of course I gotta go."

The main difference was that this was the real Devil's Castle—not the postwar-era Villa Rosa Sasazuka but a vast, opulent throne room, the very site of the Devil King and Hero's ultimate battle.

"But if we all bought our own presents for Alas Ramus, at least one of us was bound to buy the same thing for her. I was super-busy with training, so I woulda had to chisel some time out of my schedule to shop for it, too. That's why I suggested—hey, I know Alas Ramus is important, but it's not like we should shower her with gifts from the get-go. Let's just pare it down to what the girl really wants and pool our money together for it."

"Yeah. That sounds smart."

Rika wasn't sure how Urushihara would find any money to contribute to the cause, but she agreed nonetheless.

"Like, with a present, if the recipient likes it, that's great, but if she actually uses it, that's golden. You gotta go with something from the heart—that's what Ms. Kisaki taught me. But this is all such a new experience for Alas Ramus. If we surprise her with something she doesn't want, it'd be a buzzkill for both of us. So I asked Emi to try and casually ask her what kinda stuff she'd like. And then…"

Early the next morning, Emi had reported to Room 201, tears in her eyes. An alarmed Maou had asked her what was up, but she had just gone inside and asked him to summon Chiho and Suzuno at once. It was barely past sunrise, but given the way she was acting, Maou sensed it was wise to follow her instructions. Both of them came to Room 201 without complaint after having the situation explained to them.

The previous night, Emi had fulfilled her promise to Maou and casually asked Alas Ramus whether she had anything she wanted. She was a fan of corn soup, Emi knew, as well as curry. Relax-a-Bear was a big hit with her, as were small animals, and toys, and plushes, and stuff. But Alas Ramus didn't want any of that.

"She said she wanted to see everyone," Emi choked out between the sobs. "I didn't know what she meant at first—the Devil King, or Chiho, or Bell, or whatever…but it wasn't any of them."

Everyone in the room held their breath, struck by an uneasy premonition.

"She wanted to see Malkuth and all her friends. She said she didn't want anything else."

Nobody had any words to comfort her with. Her tears smashed apart any would-be conviction that something from the store would ever please Alas Ramus.

"Devil King, everyone… I was such an idiot. This entire time, that child wanted nothing more than to see Acieth and Erone again. But I turned my eyes away from that. I shut my ears from that. Wasn't that just so stupid?"

She hugged herself as she cowered down to the ground, as if cradling the Alas Ramus inside her.

"I… I was so preoccupied with myself."

A near-infinite amount of time seemed to pass. It was really just half an hour or so, but that was more than enough time to change the minds of everybody inside Room 201.

"Look… Devil King…" Emi wiped the tears and looked up at Maou. "Is it all right if I go?"

"……!"

Maou gasped. Why was she asking him for permission? Why *him*?

"I don't care about Ente Isla. No matter what kind of danger its people are facing, it doesn't matter to me. But this child is the only thing I truly care about from the heart. I can't abandon her."

Being a Yesod fragment, or fused with her holy sword, or whatnot didn't matter.

"This girl is my…"

"Ahhhhhhhh, maaaan!!"

Maou could no longer allow Emi to go on by herself. There was no way he could have Emi shoulder the punishment for all their crimes. That, at the very least, he could never forgive.

"Ashiya!" he barked, scratching his head.

"Y-yes!"

"Urushihara!"

"Uh-huh."

"Chi!"

"Yeah…"

"Suzuno!"

"Yes."

"…Emi?"

"…Devil King."

Maou lifted Emi's chin upward, toward him. They looked eye to eye.

"Look, we were *all* stupid pricks looking out for ourselves! That sound about right to you?!"

Nobody in the room tried to deny it.

"So I think I told you about Sephirot and the Sephirah back when Ashiya was kidnapped. The guy Laila and Gabriel wanted us to defeat is holding Alas Ramus's family hostage. Alas Ramus is beside herself with loneliness because she can't see them. That means there's just one thing for us to do."

After finishing the simmered kale, a bowl of rice, and a cup of instant miso soup, Maou left the empty dishes on the table and put his hands together.

"We need to bring Alas Ramus to them. I dunno if you could call them her friends, or her siblings, or her cousins, or whatever, but some grown-ups out there are treating them like crap, and we gotta whip their asses. I guess if we whip Ignora's ass, too, that'll be doing whatever Laila wants us to do, but I don't really care about that. Nothing in any of this takes higher priority than Alas Ramus."

Rika looked at her rice bowl for a moment, then lightly nodded. Now it all made sense.

"The one statement that turned it all on its head, huh?"

"Hmm?"

"That's how Chiho described it. She said you were all so comfortable with sticking around in Japan, but one word made you all change your minds."

She nodded again as she finished up her midafternoon snack and looked around the throne room she was currently sharing with Maou.

"Pretty funny one-room apartment you got here."

"You like it? This is my Devil's Castle. Not really my original one, but..."

"No? Given how you rebuilt the Shuto Expressway, I figured this would be a piece of cake for you."

Maou shook his head. "I made the outside, but the interior's been part of the demon realms for ages now. It dates from back when the Devil Overlord Satan—the Satanael guy Gabriel was talking about—descended into our realm."

He stacked up the dishes and left the table, heading for the window Rika flew out of not long ago. Rika followed him.

"The guys from heaven were able to set up shop where they are on the moon because they had those mobile colony cities. Did you hear about that?"

"A little, yeah." Rika nodded as she looked up into the sky out the window. Two moons were floating there in the middle of the afternoon.

"So Ignora and her team used the samples they got from Caiel and Sikeena to craft an immortality formula not long after they left their home planet for good. They gradually used it on themselves, gathering data and searching for a new habitable planet they could call home."

"Sounds like it could've taken forever. I mean, when I first moved to Tokyo, I looked at five apartments in one day, and that was enough to exhaust me."

"That's a lot for one day, man. You probably couldn't even figure out which was better than what by the end of it."

Rika gave this perfectly normal reaction an eager nod.

"So anyway, those guys all wound up there. They tried to rule over the Sephirot on Ente Isla before it could conjure up a second Caiel and Sikeena for them. Basically, Ignora wanted to create a second paradise for her people, but Satanael was against it. His vision was basically, like, once we find someplace and things calm down, let's undo the immortality and live in this pure new land as human beings again. But after seeing how foolish humans can be, the Ignora camp wasn't buying any of it. That Sephirot had only just chosen Ente Isla and taken root in its land; it was trying to guide the people on the planet to their own utopia. But while Satanael and Laila and a few of the angels were against it, Ignora's camp was in the majority. Can you guess why?"

"...No."

"Well, they may've been immortal, but they still feared for their lives. None of them were willing to take these bodies that never got sick or starved and just toss them away. So Satanael left. He fled with his son Lucifer and the Sephirah Yesod, the core of Ignora's immortality tech. He wanted to release the people of this new planet from the nightmare of living forever."

"Yesod... Meaning Alas Ramus and Acieth?"

"Yeah. Caiel and Sikeena formed the base of Ignora's research, and they were born from the Yesod back on their home planet. It was only natural they'd use the Yesod and Malkuth from *this* planet to continue with their research."

"This is kind of a lot to wrap my head around. I'm still dealing with the reality of this fantasy world."

"Yeah, maybe... Let's go back down for now."

"Be gentle."

Rika rode on Maou's back as he plunged down from that dizzying height once more. All so they could go wash the dishes from their meal. It would have been hilarious if it wasn't true.

While the Lord of All Demons looked for some water to wash the bowls with, Rika, a bit more clearheaded now, looked around the camp for a bit. It was arranged neatly in rows of tents from the base of Devil's Castle, overseen by a tandem effort led by General Hazel Rumack and Malebranche leader Farfarello. This was the site where humans battled bitterly against demons just a few years ago, but an alliance had been forged thanks to Ashiya and the Knights of the Great Eight Scarves, which had come under control of the demons once more. The forces were being led by Emeralda, Suzuno, Urushihara and Laila, and even Chiho to some extent.

The goals of this combined force, on the surface at least, were to dismantle Devil's Castle and withdraw all remaining demons from the area while making it look like they had been wiped out for good. In other words, it was a cleanup effort—they wanted to eliminate all trace of the demon invasion and bring any remaining hostiles back home. Most of the demons here, outside those under Farfarello's direct command, were forces that had survived life on Ente Isla ever since the first invasion.

This entire operation was treated as top secret. Maou was going around as a human being, not as a Devil King, since having him be "defeated" by the Hero Emilia would help keep confusion to a minimum should word get out about this.

"So Satanael tried to bug out of the colony, but Ignora, and Camael, and the others raked him over the coals for it. In fact, they even condemned it as yet another example of foolish human behavior. That despite their 'guiding' an entire planet's worth of people to do their bidding."

"And the people on Ente Isla didn't think anything was weird about it?"

"You kidding me? Ente Isla at the time was still a bunch of prehistoric hunter-gatherers."

"Oh, right, the people on heaven have these really long lives, don't they? The whole scale of this is amazing to me."

"Well, I'm almost done, so make sure you're taking notes. It's gonna show up on the test, so…"

As he spoke, Maou was busy washing the dishes, drying them and putting them back in their place.

"The Sephirah are all about selecting human populations that deserve to be saved, but that doesn't mean all the competing species died out or anything. So Ignora used the guys who *weren't* picked by the Sephirah and did something terrible with 'em."

"Something terrible?"

"Yeah. They modified their genes and used 'em as experimental test subjects for the immortality research they conducted after Satanael took the Yesod."

"Test subjects?!"

"Yeah, well, you can see how that kinda pissed Laila and Satanael off. It pretty much erupted into all-out war, but you know, even the test subjects wanted to keep on living. Maybe Sephirot skipped them, but we're still talking human beings, y'know? So it's not like all the modified test subjects just did what Ignora's team told them to do. Satanael rounded them all up for his side to build his numbers and also so he could give those dudes a little more protection."

Rika noticed the look of serenity on Maou's face when he referred to "those dudes"—and that his eyes were focused on the demons, the grotesque monsterlike creatures around them.

"H-hang on, Maou. Are you saying those test subjects, the ones the Sephirah didn't pick…?"

"With Yesod stolen from them, they needed something else to base their immortality research on. For their DNA sample, they picked Sikeena—in other words, the Sephirah Malkuth. That's the Sephirah that rules over physical matter, and I guess it paid off, because the test cases received an incomplete form of immortality. They could go without food as long as they wanted, their life spans increased drastically, and their bodies underwent assorted changes.

Some of 'em grew horns, some of 'em grew wings, some of 'em got tails...and some of 'em cast off the holy energy in their hearts and replaced it with something else."

He pointed out a group of demons lined up in front of a cauldron full of soup Chiho was watching over.

"So, yeah, we demons used to be human, apparently. Just a different ancestry from the humans dominant on Ente Isla now."

"Wowww," Rika half moaned. It was such an epic origin story, she didn't know how else to react. "So that story..."

"A fair amount of people know it by now. Ashiya and Urushihara, of course. Emi, Chi, Suzuno, Emeralda, and Albert. Emi's dad, Acieth, and Erone. Amane and my landlord. We had to let the higher-ups in the Federated Order and Emeralda's Holy Magic Administrative Institute on Saint Aile in on it, too, so they'd volunteer to pitch in. Also, he's not here, but I have a proxy over in the demon realms taking the throne in my place, and I told him, too. And you now, I guess."

"I kinda feel like I'm the one least impacted by it out of all of them."

"What're you talking about? History isn't written by us. It's written by people like you. People observing things one step away from the action."

"I'm honored you put it that way, but I'm just one girl in the middle of these devastating events. I have a feeling anything I could say is gonna be buried."

Rika gave Maou a closer look. This is something she was already well aware of, but the Sadao Maou in front of her wasn't a single iota different from any other human being she knew. She knew he looked like this only after he was drained of all his demonic force, but it made it easier to imagine how, at the core of every demon, there was a human being who provided the root framework.

But this presented another question. A question that made Rika wonder if Maou had ever considered it.

"But you know, why is Sephirot and the Sephirah picking one human species over the other in the first place?"

"Hmm?" Maou murmured, washing additional dishes. Rika, for

her part, was already looking at a passing contingent of Eight Great Scarves knights from Efzahan, not thinking too much about what she asked.

"I mean, all the knights here don't look any different from you or Ashiya right now. The way you just put it, your ancestors were the un-chosen ones, right? So why's Sephirot being choosy with people on Ente Isla? What are its criteria, and why does it only choose one?"

"Umm…" Maou's hands stopped. "…Maybe it's got its own reasons. God only knows, to borrow a phrase."

"Huh. Well, no matter what you'd say about it, maybe they really are just that much different from you, huh? Like on the DNA level."

Rika turned toward another group of what were clearly demons. Something about this seemed convincing to her.

"Okay, so if Ignora experimented on these guys, why are they living in the demon realms now? They were kind of like prisoners to her, weren't they?"

"Eauhhh…"

Maou winced, as if a fish bone was caught in his throat. He quickly recovered, going back to his drying and putting-away duties.

"Well, after Ignora created the sort-of prototypes for the demons, Satanael basically decided she had gone crazy. So he picked up his ball and left. He needed to get a safe distance away from Ignora's side, since they were more capable of staging a full-on tactical war than his team. He needed to round up the demons, give them protection, and use the few angels who joined his side to train them into a fighting force somewhere far away from Ignora. So Satanael created the demon realms—by which I literally mean that he basically took his part of the colony and the chunk of moon it was on and cut it away. I can't even imagine what kinda impact that had on the planet, but…ahh, Satanael was a scientist, so I'm sure he picked the exact right time to do it or whatever. Nowadays, it's a demon-infested wasteland, but at the time, it was kind of like an evacuation vessel, protecting Ente Isla from its invaders… They called it Satan's Ark."

Satan's Ark—the former domain of the Devil Overlord and the subject of myths and legends among all demons, including Maou as he attempted to unite their lands. It was literally a rescue ship, partitioned off by Satanael from his home colony.

"When I first made it to Satan's Ark, there were still records dating from Satanael's last fight with Ignora, not that I understood what they were when I first saw them." Maou paused a minute, basking in nostalgia. "But Satanael was beaten by Ignora. He died in battle. The angels with him scattered all over the place, and the poor, primitive demons with them had to flee as well. I didn't know it, but this Devil's Castle itself was actually carved out from the remains of the Satan's Ark Satanael left behind."

"Huh?!"

"You can use Gate magic to transport a whole bunch of people at once, but there are limits to it, and I wanted to save the demons capable of casting it for the Ente Isla invasion. So we used this instead. Right now, Ashiya and Urushihara are out commanding demons and knights from the Eastern Island to repair the internal workings of Devil's Castle. They're borrowing some help from Emeralda's Holy Magic Administrative Institute, too."

"Wait, are you saying this... This whole castle is a spaceship?!"

She had been told that this Devil's Castle appeared out of nowhere in the middle of Isla Centurum, the largest city in the Central Continent, and destroyed the whole place overnight. It literally crushed the city, landing right on top of it—and then Maou and the other demons rebuilt the outside to make it look more like a castle.

"We need something on this scale or else we wouldn't be able to transport all the troops we intended to have. To be honest, though, when Satanael carved out his chunk of the moon, it wasn't exactly a precision job. I kinda regret not using this thing more effectively. Hopefully I can get Devil's Castle back up in the air. That's gonna be the first step toward figuring out how to get Alas Ramus her present."

"Oh, right, you were here to give Alas Ramus that present, weren't you?"

Maou's story was on such a massive scale, beginning with the origin of his species and everything, that Rika had totally forgotten.

This massive battle, involving three worlds and a million different races, had all started simply because a little girl had a present she wanted.

"Yep. So any fight that doesn't directly involve that, I'm not gonna try too hard in. Plus, I got a training shift the day after tomorrow."

"...Sorry, come again?"

And now Maou was shifting the scale so rapidly Rika couldn't keep up.

"Huh? I said, I got my first training shift of the year in two days, so I gotta go back to Sasazuka. With Emi it's more like tomorrow morning, so *she's* gotta get back to Eifukucho tonight. Chiho's going back today—you know, she can't be away from her family *too* much during the holiday."

"Wait, what? I'm sorry, I don't really understand. Chiho! Hey, Chiho!"

"Hiiii! Sorry, can you fill in for me real quick?"

Called by Rika, Chiho enlisted a nearby demon to tend to the cauldron before running up to her. The demon was hideous, easily several times the size of a human being, but he obediently began stirring the pot after the teenage girl asked him nicely. It was comical. Given that demons didn't even need to eat, Rika wondered what this one even thought about its assigned task.

"Chiho?! Didn't you say that Maou and Emi quit their jobs at MgRonald?!"

"Huh?" Chiho's large, round eyes looked up at her. "No, I never said that."

"Sure you did! You said they 'already worked it out' or whatever."

"They did. Yusa and Maou worked out their shift schedule so they never have to be on duty here and at MgRonald at the same time."

".........Oh."

"With the Gate, they can get back to Sasazuka in about forty minutes, so they're both still working shifts at MgRonald, you know? Maybe not quite as many as before, but..."

".........Forty minutes? ...Oh."

Forty minutes could get you from Shinjuku in downtown Tokyo

to Hachioji, the final stop on the Keio line, if you boarded the express train. From Rika's home in Takadanobaba, it'd give her enough time to reach Shin-Tokorozawa on the Seibu Shinjuku line or maybe Nishi-Funabashi, the last stop on the Tokyo Metro Tozai Line. For that matter, if they boarded a Tokaido Shinkansen bullet train at Tokyo Station, they could reach Odawara, on the way to the beaches of Atami, in forty minutes. On the Tohoku Shinkansen, they'd just barely make it to Oyama, way over in Tochigi Prefecture.

"Aren't these other worlds supposed to be super far away? I mean, what the hell?!"

Rika grabbed her head and kneeled down on the floor. Looking at her, Chiho whipped out the glowing feather pen used back in Room 201.

"I can use this pen to open a Gate without any holy force. I could get one for you, too, if you like, Rika. I'm sure Laila or Gabriel could make one for you, and Emeralda could teach you how to use it in about an hour..."

"You make it sound like I'm learning how to ride a scooter! This is crazy! You're treating it like it's nothing! Over in their apartment, you were going on like I was never gonna see Emi and them all again! What the hell happened?!"

"Huh? Was that what it sounded like? I'm sorry. It was so early in the morning, I was kind of tired, and it was, like, super-cold in there. I guess it made me sound a lot blunter than I usually am. I'm sorry... Oh, and can you believe it, Maou? It got down to twenty-eight degrees in Tokyo this morning! I thought I was catching a cold for sure!"

"Wow, twenty-eight? That's pretty cold. Kinda nice how we're near the equator on this planet, huh? Makes it hard to figure out what clothing to bring, but..."

"What is this, a vacation to you?! Gimme my tears back!!"

From an impartial perspective, Rika was making perfect sense. Unfortunately, common sense was not prevalent among Maou or Chiho right now.

"Oh, hey, if you wanna borrow a scooter, by the way, I could lend you one. This is your first time in Ente Isla! If you wanna go explore the land, we still got those bikes me and Suzuno took here. I mean, we wrecked them, but I heard Albert's managed to track down all the parts we need, so I could get 'em repaired for you. It's the same type I use for MgRonald deliveries, so it's super-stable. You won't have any problem keeping it upright at all. You sure don't need a license here, either, and we got two of 'em, so maybe I could even have Ashiya show you around. He told me you helped him out a lot with his phone, so—"

"Is this really another world?! What kind of alien world has motor scooters?! What am I even doing here?! And oh, God, keep me way the heck away from Ashiya! I'm already panicking enough as it is!"

"Huh?"

"Oh, um, Maou, Rika and Ashiya kinda have some, uh, things going on right now…"

"They do? Huh. Didn't know."

He really didn't. As with their TV purchase, all he was aware of was that Rika provided Ashiya a crash course in smartphone shopping the other day.

"Boy, she looks really stressed out."

"Oh, hey, Emi."

"Yusa!"

Emi popped out from the general's tent, attracted by the sounds of Rika's agony.

"How could I *not* be stressed out by all this?!"

"Rii-Sis, what's wrong?"

And Alas Ramus was in her arms, no less. Rika didn't know whether to laugh or scream.

"I'm sorry, Alas Ramus! I'm just on the verge of losing my marbles right now! And seeing you here of all places literally just made me think I should've gotten a gift for you! As if I had the free time for any of that!"

"…Huh?"

"Yeah! Huh is right! Exactly!!"

Emi was starting to feel sorry for Rika. Handing Alas Ramus over to Maou, she gave the raging Rika an embrace from the side.

"Look, think of it this way. Let's say we had to move out to the suburbs due to some family stuff. Just pretend that the train line to our new place is over in Sasazuka. Once the New Year's season is behind us, I'll be back at my place in Eifukucho every night to sleep, and I guess Suzuno can't keep the apartment empty for too long at a time, so she'll be back in Room 202. Besides, when Chiho's over here, somebody needs to take her back home afterward. The demons need to stay here for longer, what with fixing up Devil's Castle and all, so they brought all their stuff over here, but none of our lives are really changing that much. See? Look."

She looked straight up at Devil's Castle.

"Just think of this as a really big one-room apartment, and it starts to seem a little more normal, doesn't it?"

"…You're being ridiculous."

It was a little too much for Emi to ask for. But it still brought the smile back to her face.

"You know I couldn't accept this in a zillion years. You and Maou just have all these zany surprises for me, I hardly even know what to think anymore. What does 'a big one-room apartment' even mean? That's not funny. And this apartment's a spaceship, too? It's so absurd I'm still pretty convinced it's a dream."

"Well," Maou said as he walked up to his castle, "sorry to disappoint you, but it's all real. We're going to use this Devil's Castle to attack heaven. With the Gate closed to there, that's the only way to do it." He placed a hand upon it. "After that… Well, what are we gonna do after that, Emi?"

"I dunno. We can think about it later."

Right now, Maou and Emi—or Mommy and Daddy—were working together for a common goal. But it was worth remembering that many, if not most, people on Ente Isla had no idea this battle was taking place. The tragedies engineered by Maou and his cohorts, including the destruction of Isla Centurum at the hands of his Devil's Castle, were just as vivid and true as they always were.

"I'm not a Hero any longer. If any thought passes through my mind during this battle or even after it, it's probably gonna be about how we'll spend next Christmas with Alas Ramus."

"Huh. Guess things're pretty peaceful with you after all."

"They sure are," Chiho said to Rika. "We've all worried and fought and exhausted ourselves long enough. Nobody's going to complain if we start doing a few constructive things for ourselves now."

"…Well, I'm glad you're treating it like this casual easy thing, but you do realize what Emi's starting to sound like, right? Vis-à-vis Maou?"

Rika meant it as a warning to Chiho, in a way. Chiho was ready for it.

"Oh, don't worry. I'm ready. No matter who I'm competing against, I don't think I could lose to anyone."

"Well, if you're okay with that, then fine." Rika scowled a bit. "Me, though, I dunno…"

"My liege, may I have a word?"

Suddenly, the voice of an invisible Ashiya echoed across the area. Rika reared back, cheeks bright red with shame, as the rest of them tilted their heads slightly skyward.

"What's up, Ashiya?"

"Well… Hmm? Is someone there besides Emilia and Ms. Sasaki? I sense another human being."

"Umm, nothing to worry about. What's going on?"

Chiho was shaking her head and making a giant X with both arms next to Rika. Maou gave her an odd look but got the message anyway.

"Er, yes… Well, I am afraid we have a problem."

"A problem?"

"Yes. We've learned that, as things currently stand, a full repair is no longer possible. Urushihara told me of serious problems with the engine, the transmitters, the fuel system, and almost everything else."

"We can't cover for that with magic?"

"We need to fabricate some new parts from scratch to fully fix it. I

will have Urushihara discuss it directly with you later, but that is the preliminary report I received."

"From scratch…? That stuff was made in heaven! What're we gonna do about that? It's not like they were kind enough to leave blueprints for us, right? Man, I don't remember wrecking it that badly."

"I would describe crash-landing it in the middle of Isla Centurum as 'wrecking it that badly,' personally."

Maou frowned at this evaluation. It made Emi chuckle a little.

"We might be able to bring it into the air, but if we advanced upon heaven with it, we can expect a healthy counterattack. I think we should act to eliminate as many question marks as possible beforehand."

"Yeah, but how're we gonna get the parts we need?"

"One of them's easy enough," interrupted Urushihara's voice. *"We can find it in Ente Isla's Northern Island. The other stuff, I figure we can get in the demon realms."*

"The Northern Island and the demon realms?"

"Yeah, dude. You should contact Camio and have him organize a search party for what we need. I dunno where exactly we can find 'em yet, but I know everything we need, at least."

"For real?"

Something about Urushihara's uncharacteristically serious tone of voice was lighting a fire inside Maou.

"Okay, so what are they?"

"They're called the Noah Gears," Urushihara stoically replied. *"The relics of the Devil Overlord."*

"The Noah Gears?"

"Yeah. That's what Satan…I mean Satanael called them. It's one of the few things I do remember from back then. He said they're the keys to launching Satan's Ark if they ever return to the moon."

"How do you know that's in the demon world?"

"Because heaven's looking for 'em. I think Ignora knows we need them to revive Satan's Ark. Gabriel even asked me about them once."

"Ohhh? So what are they?"

"The Nothung. The Spear of Adramelechinus. The Sorcery of the False Gold. The Astral Gem. Those four things. Satanael just had to make it a huge pain, huh?"

"Mm? Mmm."

The reasoning behind it was clear enough, however. The Nothung and the spear were mere weapons by themselves. The sorcery was just a chemical formula, the Astral Gem just a big chunk of energy. They were all unusual and wondrous relics, yes, but they were all replaceable. Only when all of them were in the right place did the Devil Overlord's bequest form the gears that drove the ark.

"Ugh… After all this time, fights from even the distant past are still affecting us to this day…"

"Yeah, pretty much."

"No, *not* pretty much, you. It was your father who did it."

"What do you want from me, man? Like it's my fault my parents screwed up my future so bad. You're a dad now, too, Maou, so try not to be as irresponsible as those guys, okay? Anyway, that's my report."

The Idea Link faded away, returning silence to the surroundings.

"Um, so the spaceship doesn't work right now?"

"Pretty much. Now we got even more junk to look for. No rest for the wicked, I guess." Maou cracked his neck a couple of times before taking a deep breath, sighing it out, and steeling his resolve. "Emi? Chi?"

"Yeah?"

"Yes!"

"It's not gonna be next Christmas."

He looked straight into the eyes of Alas Ramus in his arms.

"What, Daddy?"

"It's gonna be your birthday."

"Ooh?"

"Alas Ramus, I'm gonna have this all wrapped up by your next birthday."

"Um, and when is that, Maou?"

"When do you think?"

Maou grinned and raised Alas Ramus up toward the sky in his arms.

"Eeeeee-hee-hee!"

Everyone at Room 201 on that day had been there for the birth of Alas Ramus—that little girl, enjoying the sensation of flight in Maou's hands.

"The time limit's this summer! The next Obon festival this July in Tokyo! And I'm gonna give you the best birthday present you've ever seen, Alas Ramus!"

The bold declaration wafted its way into the air, into the afternoon overseen by the two moons in the sky.

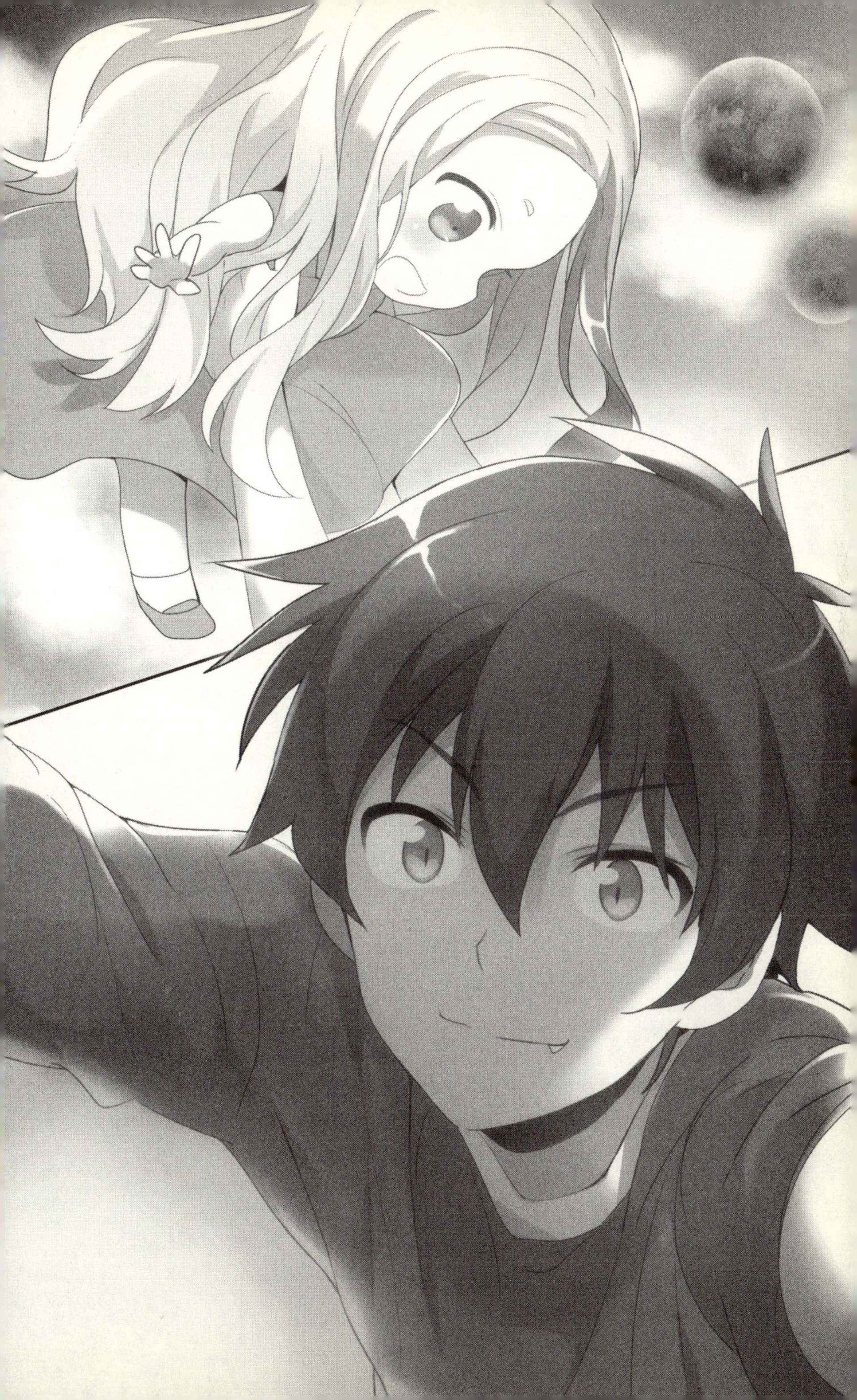

THE AUTHOR, THE AFTERWORD, AND YOU!

There are quite a few occasions in the year when it's considered acceptable to give gifts to one another. After New Year's, there's Valentine's Day in February, followed by White Day in March, where women in Japan give presents in return to the men who gave them Valentine's gifts. In the spring, you have the hat trick of Mother's Day, Children's Day, and Father's Day, along with the *ochugen* summer gift-giving tradition. No time for rest after that, though—Respect for the Aged Day comes in September, and then the year is rounded out with Christmas and the *oseibo* period. (Let's not forget birthdays and anniversaries, either.)

I doubt many people go through the effort of preparing something for every event, every year, but I'm willing to bet that most of us are on either the giving or receiving end for at least half of them. Out of them all, however, it's still Christmas presents that I have the most trouble figuring out.

It's one thing if you're a grown-up shopping for a child. It's just a matter of considering what they'd like and buying it—a book, a toy, some kind of educational thing, or maybe an electronic gadget. But what about all the presents adults buy for each other? I have no idea what the best answer is for something like that. There's no standard go-to, like a carnation for Mother's Day or chocolate for Valentine's Day or some equivalent-value sweets for White Day. For *ochugen* or *oseibo*, the standard is some kind of local produce or something the recipient and their family may find useful. Father's Day is about thanking Dad for his hard work, and Respect for the

Aged Day is about hoping your elders stay healthy for years to come; a lot of people receive trips or other presents along those lines.

But what makes for a Christmas present if neither the givers nor the receivers are devout Christians? From what I can tell, in Japan men mostly give jewelry or handbags, while women give men useful business accessories or clothing. Is that sort of thing really well suited for the Christmas season, though? I'm not so sure of that. People might counter that by saying something with a Christmassy design is best—but of course, that's going to be something wintry, so you can't use it all year, and there'll probably be some other limited-time design the very next year. At the same time, though, nobody's asking you to go into a Christmas date with your lover and bring a tree, or a roast turkey, or some fancy cake as your main present.

Christmas was never originally about celebrating individuals (like with birthdays) or bringing your feelings for other people across (like Valentine's or Mother's Day), but in modern-day Japan, it's now taken on aspects of all those holidays, leading to this crazy sense of expectation among many recipients. Sometimes, I feel like people use Christmas to say something they missed the chance on earlier that year—fathers who were gone for business on Father's Day, lovers who were too busy to celebrate a birthday, relatives you couldn't reach before now. It's your last chance to really celebrate the end of the year without all that other holiday stuff in the background. I imagine most people make up for past omissions earlier than December 25, but if you're wondering what to get someone for Christmas, maybe think about what you couldn't do for that person up to now. The answer could come more quickly than you'd think.

Volume 15 of *The Devil Is a Part-Timer* takes Christmas, which is packed with all those different thoughts and motivations, and stuffs even more complex issues into it.

With any gift, it's what's in the heart that matters first. A gift doesn't have to be a thing or something of financial value. And one thing I especially want to note is, with everyone giving their all during Christmas, I definitely don't want any gift-giving traditions associated with Halloween, which has grown in popularity in Japan lately. We've already got enough on our plates.

With that, I hope to see you all in the next volume!

IN THIS FANTASY WORLD, EVERYTHING'S A GAME—AND THESE SIBLINGS PLAY TO WIN!

No Game No Life © Yuu Kamiya 2012
KADOKAWA CORPORATION

A genius but socially inept brother and sister duo is offered the chance to compete in a fantasy world where games decide everything. Sora and Shiro will take on the world and, while they're at it, create a harem of nonhuman companions!

No Game No Life, Please! © Kazuya Yuizaki 2016 © Yuu Kamiya 2016
KADOKAWA CORPORATION

LIGHT NOVELS 1–9 AVAILABLE NOW

LIKE THE NOVELS?

Check out the spin-off manga for even more out-of-control adventures with the Werebeast girl, Izuna!